SHARK FIGHT

THE DYSTOPIAN SEA BOOK 2

SEAN-MICHAEL ARGO

SEVERED PRESS
HOBART TASMANIA

SHARK FIGHT

Copyright © 2018 Sean-Michael Argo

WWW.SEVEREDPRESS.COM

ISBN: 978-1-925840-32-2

1.

The sleek raiding vessel skipped over the murky ocean waters at a tremendous speed. The men and women on deck bared their teeth in delighted anticipation as the trading vessel grew in their sights. The trading vessel was no match for theirs. It was slow and encumbered by the weight of its cargo.

"Ready the projectiles!" The captain, a short, burly man, bellowed. A coat of black hair slick with sea salt and sweat covered his thick arms.

Chaos from the trader's vessel echoed over the waves to the raiders, fueling their every action with delight. Two crew members manned each of the four catapults aboard the deck. They loaded up their projectiles, which were composed of trash scooped from the toxic waters, a mixture of plastic and rubble ready to burn for hours after release.

The captain raised his arm, standing in the center of the catapults. He watched as the small dots of humans collected above the decks of their vessel. He waited until his ship grew near enough for them to see the destruction awaiting them.

"Fire!" His arm snapped down to his side.

Without hesitation, one man from each team lit their projectile and their partner released the catapult. Within moments the slings were reloaded, and the decks of the trading vessel were aflame. Blood-curdling screams cut through the air. The captain smirked as he watched flaming bodies dive from the top deck to the churning waters below in hopes of relief from the melting plastic adhered to their flesh.

"Prepare for receive fire!" The captain bawled.

The raiders did not need to hear this to prepare themselves. The crew members manning the catapults stood in a manner to shield themselves as best as they could behind their giant weapons while arrows rained from the dark skies all around the men. One of the men on the catapults took an arrow through the eye but like perfect cogs in a mechanism, another crew member took his place, unmoved by his dead comrade bleeding out beneath him.

The two ships were soon within meters of each other, close enough to make out the number of men on deck, close enough for the captains to see their foes head-on. Both captains released men on jet skis to fill the open waters between the vessels. The best warriors of each ship clashed with fury, bleeding into the cruel ocean below.

Traders were fierce. They were accustomed to protecting their goods, but soon this bloodbath went in favor of the raiders. The majority of traders were prepared to die defending their transports, but they were nothing compared to the cutthroat raiders who made their living by being killing machines.

The raider captain watched as his men attacked the traders with an armament of creative, grotesque weapons. They wielded chainsaws with teeth carved into hooks to peel away flesh, ball bats wound in animal spines and barbed bits of sharpened wire, make-shift cat-o-nine tails decorated with bits of glass, nails and shark hooks, and the occasional crossbow launching poisonous arrows.

The traders tried to meet the raider's battle weapons with traditional sorts, harpoons, lances, even a sword or two, but their lack of bloodlust and the training to harness that fury made them weak in the open waters. Their life spilled into the seas, staining them red. Above, on the decks of the ship, the raiding captain ordered for the remaining crew members to launch ropes across to the burning trade craft. Lines shot into the air and grappling hooks bit into the wooden railings of the trading vessel.

"Remove those lines!" The trading captain ran to remove hooks as they lashed at the sides of her vessel. *"Don't let them aboard! For God's sake, don't let them aboard!"*

The raiding captain smiled as he witnessed the other captain frantically hacking and pulling at the lines threatening her ship but there had been too many launched in quick succession and there were too few traders left alive to keep up. The raider took it upon himself to do the honors. He steadied the crossbow loaded with the hooked line, aimed, and shot it straight at the scrambling trading captain.

The hook whizzed past her, taking down her first mate. She screamed in fury and doubled her efforts to prevent the raiders from boarding her ship and ending them all. Some of the men started to slip through, crawling across the open waters using the lines. Her men continued to cut lines as she took on the boarding raiders with a sword in one hand and a dagger in the other.

Just as all hope seemed to be slipping, the vigor of the raider's attack slowed. It took the captain of the trading ship a moment to realize what had stolen the attention from the assault. She thought, just for a moment, she could win.

It was then she noticed the dark masses flooding the horizon towards them.

Action on both vessels stilled as they each tried to make out what threat closed in on them. The raiding captain pulled his spyglass from within his coat pocket and stared through it.

Careening towards them at high speed was an army of Panzer Fish.

The raiding attack had suddenly been transformed into utter stillness at the sight of the dreaded cultists surrounded by at least fifty mutated sharks working in tandem. The sharks didn't attack the nihilistic marauders who worshiped them. As if under some spell, they cut through the water alongside the Panzer Fish. Every man stalled in horror.

No one had witnessed anything like this before. Both captains were filled with dread as they watched the approaching army. The Panzer Fish were deadlier than the raiders simply for their suicidal lack of self-preservation and the beasts that were their servants. They didn't care who of the two ships they were swooping down on, escorted by their fearsome army of hungry sharks, was victim or who was attacker, both ships were now prey.

The men and women battling in the open waters between the two vessels turned their full attention to the army of cultists and mutant sharks approaching them and within moments they were fighting alongside one another against the mutual enemy. The sharks outnumbered the bodies in the water two to one. Screams of men being torn apart by sharks echoed up from the swells.

The Panzer Fish wasted no time on the handful of people fighting the beasts below, leaving them to the sharks. They divided forces and boarded the vessels.

The raiding captain spared a look across the water at the trading ship as thick plumes of black smoke blocked most light from the sky, looking for the trading captain. Her screams called his eyes to the aft end of the vessel.

He should not have looked.

Two Panzer Fish were holding her as others lined up excitedly to take violent turns with her.

The captain looked away, down into the water between the two vessels where body parts bobbed atop water where his men fought just a moment ago.

The cries of sailors fighting, the ring of steel and the smell of blood overwhelmed him. With one last burst of energy, the captain screamed to the heavens and fought until he could fight no more.

2.

Bard kept his eyes trained on the great leviathan, his hair plastered to his face from the rain, shivering beneath soaked clothes. It wouldn't be much longer.

Drucilla's lips were pale from the wet and cold. "We're almost there!" She cried into the gales spraying around them.

Abigail didn't wait for another order. She her hook fly from the nearby boat. Her powerful legs propelled her from the bow of the lancing boat and connected her to the slick, armored hide of the leviathan. Bard jerked upright when he saw her feet slip and she dangled helplessly from the rope attached to her hook.

Acting instinctively, Bard shot his own hook over the far side of the whale and jumped, his feet landed firmly on its flesh. Abigail stabilized herself against him, planting her feet securely. The leviathan began to turn in their favor and they took the opportunity and ran with the motion. Abigail unsheathed her blade and dragged it behind her as they fled, cutting into the creature's top layer of flesh and fat. No communication was needed. At just the right moment, eyes fixed on the horizon, both sets of legs pushed away from the beast. Abigail landed in the lancing boat first. Bard nearly slipped on the bow, but her hand jutted out to catch him just in time.

A second after they leapt from the mighty beast it dived down into the depths of the ocean. Bard was thankful to have such skilled rowers, accustomed to the adrenaline-infused whims of their shipmates.

He looked at Drucilla. She was fuming. Her eyes deadlocked onto Abigail, burning with anger at Abigail's reckless and premature maneuver. Abigail intentionally avoided looking in her direction. Everyone upon the *Penny Dreadful* knew how they could get with one another.

Morgan and Kalak rode up next to the boat on their jet skis. Morgan held her bat over the handlebars, leaning into the rain, willing her vehicle to move faster. Kalak stood tall, his bulky frame overcrowding the small stand-up jet ski. His lip turned in a slight smirk as he approached us and saw Bard and Abigail had switched boats.

"Couldn't help yourself, could ya?" Kalak's booming laugh echoed the thunder and lightning crashing around us.

The rope attached to the leviathan suddenly stopped uncoiling from the boat. There was a moment of tension when the line slack as the great whale returned to the surface for air. Morgan and Kalak prepared their weapons and positioned themselves so they could defend the leviathan from sharks and other predators.

Abigail was ready long before the whale broke the surface. The rest of the world was invisible to her as she focused on where she planned to hit the whale when it rose to the surface, water sheeting from it's form. Her hand jolted and released her harpoon at the perfect moment.

Abigail's harpoon sank between the armored plates of the leviathan and she was lost in the moment. Bard held his breath until she once again became aware of her surroundings.

Drucilla was staring at her again, but this time it was with the smug, pursed lips of someone proving a point. Abigail looked around not noticing that Drucilla's harpoon had landed first, but the rest of the crew had. Abigail growled and turned to Bard, who couldn't help but laugh at her and shrug. Abigail would be peeved for weeks knowing it was Drucilla's hook that outshot hers.

The first hunt of the season was always like this. The captain was especially prudent, so far from their catch goal. Each member got competitive. Eagerness struck them and boiled their blood. The love for the hunt overwhelmed them. Wet and cold as it was, there was a familiarity to it. Even Kalak and Morgan seemed to fight the sharks harder than usual. The first hunt was important. Who won was important. For weeks after each kill, they'd talk about whose hook or lance did what until the next leviathan was spotted, but the first hunt was still rehashed until the hulls were full and emptied again.

Blood pooled from the holes the lancers left on the side of the massive whale. The sharks crowded in as everyone worked on the leviathan. Morgan and Kalak kept a running score of who killed more of the ocean predators.

"Eight!" Kalak screamed as his chainsaw ripped through the skull of one trying to snap at the flukes of the whale.

"Bullshit! You counted in at six just a second ago!" shouted Morgan, who was a wrecking ball with her spiked bat, weaving in between the aquatic monsters wantonly bashing in their heads. Her face, arms, and torso were covered in shark blood, brain matter, and more than a few teeth marks from bites that didn't quite stick.

It took another two hours for the ship to get to them. The rain had stopped by then but they were soaking wet and still had to look forward to the processing of the massive creature. There was enough carnage floating in the waters to keep the shark feeding frenzy focused on cannibalizing their own dead, leaving the well-protected leviathan relatively unmolested.

Drucilla shouted orders. "Morgan. Bard. Start melting!" She barked as he and Abigail clambered up the ladder and boarded the *Penny Dreadful.*

"Aye, aye, Ma'am," Morgan grinned and gave a bow before spinning on her heels and leading the way.

Bard grimaced, he hated melting down blubber, in his opinion it was one of the worst jobs, well, except retrieving oil from the head of the whale, of course. Nothing reeked worse than that. The blubber still smelled horrid when boiled down. It was part of the life of a whaler though. No matter where you went on the ship, the stench wouldn't go away until they'd finished working and cleaning the ship.

"How many did you get?" Bard asked Morgan.

"Forty-three in total!"

"Jesus, I remember when there'd maybe be ten warming into a Leviathan."

"Yeah, well," Morgan shrugged, "Me too." Morgan looked down at the boiling pot. It wasn't like her to get quiet. "What do you think's causing it?"

"Causing what?" I asked.

She looked up at me, her knees spread wide apart with balanced her weight on the arm draped over her thigh. "It's just that I've been hearin' things, y'know?" She pulled the bandana down from over her face for a moment and rubbed the bridge of her nose. "A lot of people have been talkin', and it seems like the shark populations have increased dramatically since we offed the Mega."

"Morgan, that's just—"

"I know, super-fuckin'-stition," she pulled the bandana back up to shield herself from the smell, "but I ain't ever seen nothin' like today. If it wasn't for Kalak, we would've been fucked."

"It's a good sign, right? More sharks mean more food, right?"

"If we can beat them off. This keeps up the day we get overwhelmed is coming."

"Hm. Should we say anything to Drucilla?"

"She's got enough on her plate. 'Sides, we're the best," Morgan's eyes lit up with excitement.

3.

Anand walked the various make-shift docks connecting the small structures of his village. The sky stretched out in soft hues of light blue overlaid by strips of gauze-like clouds. He stopped suddenly as a small child ran out before him to the edge of the dock. He watched with curiosity as she paid no mind to him, knelt over the side of the walkway and pulled a handful of gigantic mussels from the underside of the structure.

"Don't eat those," he warned. The little girl looked up at him with large brown eyes, "They'll make you sick."

"I know," she retorted before turning back to the mollusks.

Anand watched as the child scurried around a corner and returned with a crab pot under one arm. He leaned up against the opposing wall, wanting to ensure she wouldn't do anything dangerous. The child laid the crab pot down. Her hands moved quickly to remove the bait bag and toss the mussels inside. She threw the baited sack to the dock and squealed with delight as she stomped on the shells, crushing them open with her worn boots. Within minutes, the child prepared the pot and let it fall to the depths below attached by a large rope.

"You gonna be here a minute?" She asked Anand.

"Nah."

"Why you standin' there then? If you gonna watch me, you might as well watch my pot a minute. I need to pee."

Anand shrugged his shoulders. The little girl ran off. Her boots clanked against the hard wood of the docks. It was a beautiful day, and he enjoyed the view of the waters stretched out before him. Within a few moments, the little girl returned. Her nose ran from the crisp morning sea breeze. She looked up at him and wiped the snot away with the back of her forearm.

"Thanks."

"It's no pro—" Anand's voice trailed off as he spotted something unusual approaching on the horizon.

The little girl glanced over her shoulder, following Anand's gaze. On the horizon, a dark, uneven line started to form.

"What is it?" The little girl asked.

"Nothin' good, where are your parents?"

She shook her head. Another orphan just trying to catch a meal. Anand was about to open his mouth when a man ran past them screaming at the top of his lungs.

"Panzer Fish are coming!"

The sharp cries of women filled the air. Bells began to clang out from business porches. The little girl looked up at Anand, her eyes bulged with fear. He could see the slight tremble of her hands.

"We gotta get out of here!" Anand tried to grab her sleeve to lead her, but she tore free.

"Not without my pot!"

"There's no time," Anand insisted. The little girl started to cry as she frantically pulled at the pot weighted down in the ocean's depths.

"Please, help me!" she cried as she saw the cult flotilla grow larger and more distinct on the horizon. "I'll starve if I lose it!"

Anand thought about abandoning her, but he couldn't bring himself to run off without her. It would take her forever to pull the pot from the water by herself. He let out a growl of frustration and helped her retrieve the cage from the sea.

With the both of them working, it came up faster, but it was still taking too much time. Anand kept stealing glances up at the horizon. He could see the dorsal fins of sharks protruding from the waters in his purview. The color slipped from his cheeks as he saw this. A swarm of sharks accompanied a small army of Panzer Fish cultists sailing lightweight catamarans. A raiding party.

"You have to let it go," Anand screamed at the girl.

"I can't! I can't!"

"Look! I'll—," Anand dropped the line, "I'll barter you a new one. We need to get the fuck out of here."

The girl stopped fussing about her pot when she finally saw the severity of the situation. The marauders approached at high speeds. She looked at the crab cage in a moment of nostalgia before releasing the line and turning to run.

"Follow me!" she shouted at Anand.

Anand followed her, jutting between buildings until she encouraged him to scale atop a roof.

"Where are you taking us?" he asked.

"To my secret place!"

There was a small hatch atop the building. Anand looked around him and saw the cultists mounting the docks surrounding and connecting the small floating village, tossing women and children indiscriminately into the blue waves as they encountered them. It took mere seconds for the victims to become meals for the tremendous, mutated sharks. Women and children were valuable commodities to the pirates who prowled these waters, and yet for the insane cultists they were just so much chum.

The little girl pulled at him to hurry down. She sprinted to the opposite end where a pile of rubbish blockaded the entrance to a dogged down steel door.

"Help me," the little girl said as she threw the heaps of trash away from the door.

The footsteps of cultists could be heard moving above. The second the door was cleared enough, the little girl pushed it open and slammed it just as fast behind Anand. The sound of the door crashing shut echoed throughout the building. Anand cringed at the sound and looked up to the rooftop in fear. The sounds of the boots above quickened. He heard the hatch tear open with a clatter. He looked back at the little girl. It was a panic door. She turned the heavy steel mechanism as fast as she could. He watched as she secured the thick steel door with practiced speed.

Just as the locks clicked, something slammed hard against the other side of the door, causing the little girl to scream in surprise and jump back.

"We're fucked," Anand tore at his hair as he listened to the cultists attempting to break in.

"No, we're not, I promise." The little girl was calm after regaining composure. "My dad used to work here and built this for me before he died. It's bullet and fireproof. It's the safest place in our whole village. That's why I hafta hide it with all that gross trash when I don't have it locked from inside. My daddy showed me that."

Anand was amazed. He couldn't believe his luck. To think if he had rejected her help they probably would have both died. The room was the size of a large vault with random items scattered about, blankets, bits of food, clothing. It had windows with drawn curtains, and a periscope in the far corner. The little girl approached the periscope and peered through it. The sounds of bullets hitting the steel door echoed throughout the chamber.

"What are you looking for?" Anand asked.

The little girl didn't reply. Instead, she ran to the opposite side of the room and flicked a switch. Within a few moments, Anand heard the sounds of bodies falling just outside of the vault doors.

"What did you do?" He asked.

"Daddy was good at a lot of things. I checked to make sure there were only cultists in the rooms outside, and then I set off a contraption he built me for protection. I didn't want them to warn the rest of their people."

Anand was shocked. The little girl pushed past him again. This time she went to raise the blinds.

"No, no, no!" Anand tried to stop her.

She shrugged him off. "Relax; they are double sided. We can see through, but they only see a shoddy reflective mural on the other side. Daddy was an engineer before the Mega took him and his ship down below."

The blinds opened up. From where they hid they could see the whole village. It was in complete chaos. One of the far off structures burned, sending black plumes of smoke up to the heavens. A family of seven ran out screaming. The father and eldest sons locked in a losing battle with the Panzer Fish as their family tried to make it safely from their adjoining docks to the central parts of the village.

The scene sprawled out around them. The cries of the cult's victims did not penetrate the thick steel casing. Some men fought bravely, doing what they could, and though everyone on the water generally carried a weapon, the Panzer Fish were simply leagues ahead of the common folk in terms of combat skill and sheer bloodlust. The majority of the villagers, try at they might, were overpowered by the cruelty and sheer berserker fury of the attacking marauders.

Anand looked down at the little girl. Her eyes were wide and fixed on the horrific scene. Her small arms wrapped around herself in a secure embrace.

"You shouldn't watch this," Anand said.

The little girl looked up at him. Her eyes were wet, but no tears streamed down her cheeks, "And what, pretend it's not happening?"

There was nothing Anand could say to that. She was right. The violence unfolding was part of life, and no amount of ignoring could save them from the truth of what was happening to the village. Half of it was burning to the ground. It was hard to tell how many of their people had already died. Anand wondered if anyone other than them would even survive. He couldn't help but question whether the villagers would survive against the onslaught, as he could see the mutated sharks shattering the small crafts and jet skis some of the villagers managed to launch in an attempt to escape.

"Look!" The child's voice cut sharp through the air with excitement.

Anand followed her finger's direction to the horizon. An armored ship approached their village. Her bright multi-colored, silk sails carried the large cargo vessel at high speeds to the villagers. An entourage of hunting and lancing boats accompanied by three people on stand-up jet skis proceeded to their rescue.

4.

The *Penny Dreadful* was destined for Atoll Blue Stone when they spotted the ominous, black vortex of a floating village on fire. Captain Dru scaled up to the Crow's Nest to get a look for herself. Down below, far out on the horizon, a tiny village fought against a small army of Panzer Fish cultists.

"Look in the water Captain," The crew member standing by directed her sight by moving the eyeglass down to the water. A swarm of sharks tore at the buoys and hodge-podge of floatation devices keeping the village aloft on the water. One of the Panzer Fish tossed a villager into the swarm. The red sea churned violently as the swarm averted its attention to the helpless man.

Captain Dru passed the spyglass over to her shipmate. "Thank you," she murmured as her brain processed the severity of the situation below.

Most captains would choose to change course. They would decide to shy away from the slaughter. Captain Raj has never been that sort of captain, and Drucilla had no intention of being different from the man whose boots she now filled. The sight of the sharks and cultists working together made her stomach churn. The Panzer Fish were terrors, for sure, but they usually attacked smaller prizes and in smaller numbers. Never had Drucilla seen them carry out an open, organized attack on an entire village before.

Drucilla slid down the ropes and landed on the deck of the ship. "Man the hunting and lancing boats!"

There was a moment's pause as the crew startled from their mesmerized stares out at the horizon before snapping to the captain's orders. "Bard! Kalak! Morgan!" Abigail snapped for help readying one of the hunting boats.

"Kalak. Morgan. You will lead the lancing and hunting boats into the shark swarm and distract the cultists on the north end of the village. Bard and Abigail, I want you to keep your boat as far south as possible. Once the Panzer Fish are distracted, I want you to coordinate the evacuation of the villagers. As soon as there are no boats on the docks, I will assume there are only Panzer Fish on the actual structure and," Drucilla grinned, "we will rain down on them like the wrath of God."

Morgan squealed with delight, "I'm better on a jet ski, Dru." Morgan looked up at her captain with faux pouting lips and pleading eyes.

"Absolutely not, it's too reckless with that shark swarm, that's like riding straight into a feeding frenzy. That's how even the best sharkers die," Drucilla glanced over her shoulder at the army attacking the small village, "We've never encountered these numbers before. Stay in the boats."

The crews moved in practiced silence. Kalak and Mr. Pit took charge of the small flotilla of boats. Abigail and Bard occupied the hunting ship and kept to the edge of the formation with the fastest rowers and the least amount of men. It took mere minutes to be on the water, en route to the village with harpoons, lances, and weapons in hand. The *Penny Dreadful* followed close behind with her silk sails billowing in the favorable winds.

"ARCHERS!" Drucilla's heavy boots trod with determination, up and down the decks of the ship, "Ready yourselves!"

Five men and women rushed below decks and reappeared with their quills and two types of bows in hand. The archers were a new installment under Drucilla's command. After being seemingly helpless against the megalodon, Kaiku, Drucilla had amplified the *Penny Dreadful's* long-range assault tactics. Other crew members followed behind the first set of archers with boxes of ammo.

Drucilla stood behind the archers. "Aim for the sharks first! Once Bard and Abigail evacuate the villagers, switch out! Understood?"

"Aye, aye," a unanimous response charged through the air.

As Abigail and Bard approached with the other boats, the sharks swarmed in around them. Weaving in between them, Morgan rode solo on a jet ski, wantonly bashing mutated sharks in passing.

"Damn it, Morgan!" Captain Dru cursed under her breath as she watched the woman lean into a turn from the decks. The tips of

Morgan's pigtails dragged across the water's surface before she straightened herself up. Wild laughter ripped through her.

By the time the first line of lancing boats reached the shark swarm, the sharks had managed to destroy the gas bladders and flotation buoys on the north side of the village. The makeshift shanties fell into the oscillating waves. Some of the occupants attempted to fight. Other villagers fell to the swarm of sharks. The lancing boats tried to pull out anyone struggling for survival in the waters, but it was absolute chaos and carnage. More than one of the people the crew tried to save came up with their lower bodies ripped to shreds.

"Ignore survivors in the water!" Mr. Pit ordered. The order echoed from vessel to vessel. The sharks had already killed the men and women in the water. No amount of first aid would be able to patch their wounds. They were beyond help.

Back on the ship, Drucilla walked behind her archers. Riddle appeared above decks. Her arm mount was bare and she cradled an arrangement of different mechanical arm attachments with her remaining arm. Vladimir followed behind with a box.

"Where do you want us?" Riddle reported to Captain Drucilla.

"Here, mid-deck. Focus on picking off the Panzer Fish."

"Vould you like I should focus on ones closest to Southside?" Vladimir asked.

"Aye," Drucilla gave a curt nod, "Drive those bastards north. Be cautious; we do not want to scare the villagers into their arms."

Vladimir nodded. The tinkerer aided Riddle with setting up her newest arm attachment. It was designed with sniper sights and a tripod to balance on the ship's banister for support. Vladimir followed suit with another weapon of his making. Together they started strategically picking off the Panzer Fish most likely to obstruct their plans.

5.

Abigail and Bard reached the docks with little issue, guarded by the entourage of lancing and hunting vessels. Three Panzer Fish met them as they set foot on the floating docks connecting the village's structures. Abigail drew her swords and attacked with gusto. The cultists were brutal killers, but they lacked the speed and grace of the warrior woman. Abigail was a bladed cyclone, dodging one attack and slicing two separate attackers with the momentum of her swords while Bard worked with one of the few guns, a revolver, with bullets the ship owned. An altered bayonet protruded from the tip of the barrel. In the blink of an eye his five point blank shots had put three cultists on the deck, and a fourth unable to stop Bard from piercing him with the bayonet.

"Blue Stone follow me!" Bard yelled at the horrified men, women, and children running from their homes and businesses in the chaos. "Not you," he barked, snagging a young man by the collar as he tried to make it to the hunting vessels waiting to transport the survivors to the *Penny Dreadful*, "You're fast, go find spread the word that we are on this side!"

The *Penny Dreadful's* crew prevented all the men and a few women able to fight from boarding the rescue boats, allowing only mothers and children to board. A middle-aged man tried to force himself aboard. The burliest of the rowers stood up and pushed him back, taking responsibility for acting the part of a bouncer. It was a harsh sort of triage, but one that the presence of the Panzer Fish demanded. Every body that would fight was needed to hold the line.

"You stand there and fight!" the rower looked at the man with cold eyes. He pressed the man back with the flat of his palm. The man looked around at the carnage. He tightened his grip on the shovel in his hand and swallowed hard.

"All able bodies to me!" Abigail screamed over the growing collection of villagers. A small group of would be fighters gathered alongside Abigail and Bard to protect the evacuation party from the oncoming Panzer Fish.

As Bard, his nearly spent revolver now holstered, turned to pass a little girl over to the towering rower a bat a bat slammed against his shoulder sent him stumbling forward. The Panzer Fish had exploded from the water to swing with the bat, and followed up with a swift kick across Bard's knee. Bard fell backwards, staring up at the bat raised above his head aiming to crash down on his face. Blood dripped over the Panzer's crazy eyes and pooled around the gums lining his sadistic smile. Bard looked around frantically for something to use as a weapon before remembering his pistol, and at the last moment he drew and fired the final round through the cultist's face. Blood spilled from the round mark of a bullet hole in the Panzer's forehead and he toppled to the ground on top of the prone whaler. Bard scrambled for his gun, which had skidded over the dock's boards, hoping he didn't lose the valuable piece of hardware.

Morgan was fierce in the open water. She was accustomed to navigating between raging sharks on her stand up jet ski. It was an extension of her body. Morgan armed herself with her notorious kill-bat and a collection of small knives secured to her person. She stayed close to the lancing and hunting boats, watching diligently for the safety of her teammates. Her bat smashed in the heads of shark after shark, ripping through their armored plates with the barbs and spikes lining her bat.

One shark leaped from the water next to her, jaws open and ready to crush her. Morgan spun her jet ski to come close alongside the creatures head, slamming her bat into the bracket across her handlebars. She drew her knife and plunged the blade into the beast's eye, continuing to navigate the waters with her free hand, using the forward motion of the jet ski to pull the blade through the beast's body and lay it open across the sea. A primitive war call shrieked from her lips and carried over the seas to the cultists.

Seeing Morgan's close call caused Kalak to be distracted for a moment. One of the sharks tried to rip a chunk out of the boat he navigated and a rower dropped one of his oars. The rower snatched up a lance and pierced through the beast before any real damage came to the vessel. Kalak looked at the bite missing from the top edge of the boat, sobered himself, and continued to hack away at the sharks closest to him with his chainsaw.

From the bow of the ship, Drucilla watched the battle through her spyglass. Two boats full of people had already been transported back to the *Penny Dreadful*, unloaded, and were returning to collect the last of the men fighting alongside Bard and Abigail.

"PREPARE SEATED BOWS!" Drucilla ordered.

Like clockwork, the archers changed weapons. They perched upon elongated crates moved from nearby. The bows were designed to hook under their feet, leaving both arms to pull the bowstring to their chest before releasing. There were hundreds of arrows prepared while the crew waited for the leviathan season to begin. The archers strung their bows and positioned them at the proper angle to rain down on the village ahead.

"PREPARE TO FIRE!"

The archers waited for the order. Each archer had a partner to help them load faster, then to relieve them when their cores were too worn to continue. Drucilla watched for the last of the villagers to evacuate. Bard and Abigail's boat joined the others in the shark swarm.

"FIRE AT WILL!"

The whistling sound of arrows releasing from her decks answered Drucilla's order. The second wave was already loaded and fired by the time the first bolts fell upon the Panzer Fish. It was a bloodbath. The whalers knew their work.

Drucilla watched her new hunting tactics perform wickedly well against the dreaded cultists. Wave after wave fell with arrows thudding into their bodies. There was nothing they could do. She scanned the village for any missing survivors. To her relief, it appeared anyone still occupying the town had enough sense to take cover. Watching the cultists perish beneath the arrows onslaught was like watching an insect squashed beneath the weight of a shoe as the seamless waves of arrows darkened the skies above the shark swarm.

No quarter asked and none given.

Bard and Abigail climbed about the boat with Kalak. Abigail joined Mr. Pit in the fight against the swarm while Bard took up his harpoons, focusing on the unarmored sides closest to the bellies of the sharks. The impact of the hook setting reverberated up his shoulder but with the flick of a spring loaded switch, the line would reel back in with such whirring force that the shark would flip upside down in the water. It was going to be a hard fight to get through this madness and back aboard the whaleship.

One of the hooks landed an enormous shark as the intelligent beast maneuvered in just the right manner to lodge the harpoon in its thick armored plates. Too late, Bard tried to retrieve the spear but the hook was stuck in the huge beast. The shark swam in the opposite direction, the sudden jolt of the line yanking him into the icy, churning waters.

Morgan witnessed Bard fall into the ocean. She redirected her course with faster speed than any boat could. She let out another war cry and thrust herself into the middle of the action. Her jet ski stayed close to Bard in an attempt to protect him as Kalak ordered the lancing boat to get to him. Morgan was in a violent fury, beating and slicing the sharks threatening Bard's life.

Bard fought to stay above the churning waves as Morgan tore around him, screaming and hacking in an effort to keep the sharks at bay. Both of them knowing that in seconds one of the multitude of sharks would get through, and he would be done for. Bard fought to keep his head above water as he struggled to get the knife from his hip sheath. His fingers wrapped around the hilt as the sharks closed in. He whipped the blade out as one shark made it past Morgan. The other harpoon slipped off his shoulder sank down to the fathoms below. It seemed hopeless to try fighting the huge shark but as it came toward him, he vowed to bury the knife hilt deep in the creatures eye before it took him into the bloody darkness.

Wave after wave of salt water crashed into him, obstructing his view and choking him. The beast's mouth opened wide before him and Bard closed his eyes to shut out the inevitable even as he thrust outwards with his blade. But instead of jaws clamping down on him or his blade sinking into flesh, his knife hit only air as hands suddenly grabbed onto his clothing and lifted his waterlogged body from the sea. It was Kalak pulling him into the boat.

Morgan was atop the attacking shark, having apparently leaped from her jet ski, abandoning it, to attack the shark threatening to devour Bard. Morgan's blade fell and rose over and over, stabbing as she rode the gigantic shark, her blade finally becoming lodged just above its dorsal fin. The beast flailed as it swam around to the other side of the boat. Bard struggled to get to his feet and help as fast as he could to help but by the time he succeeded, another shark had emerged. The second shark sank its jaws into Morgan's leg.

"MORGAN!" Kalak screamed. His chainsaw met the face of the shark she rode. He tried to reach out to her, to pull her onto the boat and away from the shark that had clamped down on her leg. His eyes locked with hers even as a third shark exploded out of the water behind her, its jaws open wide.

"Love you," Morgan mouthed, all bravado gone in an instant, and afraid for the first time in her short and brutal life as her fingertips grazed Kalak's.

Then the shark's jaws snapped shut across her shoulders and the two beasts ripped her down into the darkness below, all of them disappearing into the churning red waves.

Sounds of anger and anguish swept across the lancing and hunting vessels. The fierceness of every crew member doubled. This was no longer a rescue mission. This was revenge.

Kalak spun into a blind fury as he leapt from the boat and splashed down next to Morgan's discarded jet ski. Moments later he was astride it, his chainsaw ripping through shark after shark. Mr. Pit's War Hammer fell over and over, each time returning covered in gore. The two rescue boats returned filled with able fighting men. Within minutes the Panzer Fish were either dead or retreating from the *Penny Dreadful's* attack. The sharks, sensing the severity of the situation, also retreated, a singular oddity that would have put a cold fear in the heart of every man and woman present, had they not been so focused upon the battle at hand. The lancing and hunting boats pursued the shark swarm until they finally outran the vessels. Kalak was the last to return, hours later, paddling his jet ski with the flat of his chainsaw after exhausting the modest oil reserves of both the weapon and the ride.

6.

The villagers eventually unloaded from the safety of the *Penny Dreadful*. The few fires burning were extinguished by the survivors. Women and children led a procession of presenting mementos of gratitude and tribute to Captain Dru. Although the village was small, they managed to bring what food, clothes, and supplies they could afford. Despite how most captains would conduct themselves, Drucilla decided to present an allotment of oil and dried meat from the last leviathan hunt to the survivors. It was not much, but she thought of how they would need what they could get.

The last two citizens waited for the line of thankful villagers to leave. Drucilla stood in front of Anand and the small child. The little girl struggled with a small bundle tucked under her arm. Captain Dru stood stoically as the girl approached her. The child fidgeted, shifting the bundle's weight from one arm to the next. Drucilla looked down at her, waiting to see what it was she needed.

"Spit it out," Dru demanded as the girl took a nervous glance back at Anand.

"I would like to work for you, ma'am."

Drucilla studied the girl. She was sturdy, yet small. "And what makes you think you could provide any service to my crew? Go home, child. Did you not see what happened today?"

"Yes, ma'am, I did. I want to be like her. The one on the jet ski. No more hiding."

Drucilla's eyes softened at the mention of Morgan. She recognized the spirit blazing in the child's eyes. Captain Dru looked up at Anand.

"And you? I lost crew today, so there are bunks to fill."

"Yes, I want to help," Anand replied.

Drucilla thought a moment. Anand was slender and appeared weak. She could see the marks of malnourishment in his cheeks.

"Have you ever fought a shark before? Thrown a harpoon or tied a sailor's knot?"

"No, ma'am," Anand shook his head, "But I can learn."

Drucilla stepped aside to allow them to move up the gangplank. As they passed, Drucilla's words stalled them for a moment.

"You will most likely die if you do not turn back now. We sail hard waters and I will suffer no slackers on my vessel, understood?"

"Y-yes, ma'am," the child spoke.

Drucilla followed them on board. The *Penny Dreadful* would not be staying in the village overnight. The men and women under her command worked to prepare the ship to get underway. The small girl and Anand stood awkwardly upon the deck. The crewmen moved around them as if they were not there at all.

"You two," Drucilla's voice caused the child to start. They turned around to face their new captain. "I am Captain Drucilla. You will follow me down to my quarters, and we will discuss your assignments."

Mr. Pit appeared at Drucilla's side. He raised his eyebrows at the orphan and young man. Dru led the way below decks to the captain's quarters. She sat down, facing the door, with Mr. Pit at her side just as her father had done before her. With a wave of her open hand, she gestured for the two to take a seat in the remaining chairs.

"Let me see your hands, child."

The little girl raised her hands up revealing her delicate fingers. Drucilla took them into hers and actually pulled the child across the table, so she could inspect them closer.

"Make a fist around my fingers and squeeze as hard as you can." Drucilla slipped two fingers into the open palms of the child's hands. The girl obeyed her command.

"Good. You will be Vladimir's new assistant. You will wake with the others in your berthing and report to him immediately after. You will not go to chow or bathe or dillydally beforehand, understood?"

The little girl nodded, and Drucilla released her hands. She looked at Anand once again. Her intense eye contact made sweat bead at his hairline. He shifted nervously beneath her scrutinizing gaze.

"You are no shark fighter that is for certain. What can you offer me?"

Anand hardly let Captain Drucilla finish before he let out, all in one rushed exhale of breath, "I promise I'll learn anything. I can do whatever you want. If I'm not strong enough, I can cook and clean and work until I am. And if I need to fight before I am, I will risk death to prove to you I am worthy of your crew."

Drucilla narrowed her eyes at Anand, "Why are you so eager to lose your life eh, especially after getting it back from the Panzer Fish so soon?"

Mr. Pit leaned in, glaring down at the villager. Anand straightened up and took a deep breath. His fingers gripped at his trousers, just above the knee, squeezing the fabric and then releasing.

"You don't understand what it is like there," Anand looked down at his hands. "I don't have any friends," he looked back up at them, "or family. There is nowhere to go. There is nothing for me there. My hovel of a home was taken by one of the fires. I barely found the resources and work to eat. Please," he begged.

"I see something in you," Drucilla said, "But I am not sure it is useful to me."

Anand exhaled a heavy sigh. His head fell to his chest.

Drucilla continued, "You will be at Mr. Pit's side until we accept you as part of our crew and determine the best place for you. You will sleep in his quarters. You will eat when he eats. You will obey his every command as if your life depends on it," Drucilla paused and made sure he met eye contact, "Because it does."

Anand gave a weak smile as he looked at Mr. Pit. Mr. Pit was menacing. His size alone was enough to intimidate anyone.

"You'll not leave my side," Mr. Pit stated flatly.

"Is this understood?" Drucilla waited for Anand to nod in agreement before she continued, "Tonight we will mourn for the lost. You two will be present, but you will not talk to anyone unless you are answering someone else, understood. I want you to be invisible. You will not stare or judge. You will listen. Mr. Pit will take charge of you now. Dismissed."

7.

Night fell over the ocean, covering the waves in dark velvet. Only the occasional twinkling of a star penetrated the softening darkness with a touch of brilliant white light. Massive brass bowls filled with burning whale oil illuminated the bow of the ship. The world was silent except for the occasional splash of a creature and the gentle lapping of the sea against the sides of the boat.

Kalak stood in front of the *Penny Dreadful's* crew gripping onto what appeared to be an article of Morgan's clothing. Tear streaks ran through the dried blood and grime staining his face. Skullcaps slipped from heads out of respect and mourning.

"Morgan," Kalak took a deep breath to calm the tears triggered by the sound of her name on his lips. He exhaled and tried again. "She..." Kalak's face turned dark red. The fearsome shark fighter struggled to control his emotions. He twisted the fabric tighter in his hands, glanced once up at the crowd, then walked away from the center of their attention.

After a second, Abigail stood up. "Morgan was a hell of a sharker. God knows she pissed me off, and we fought more than anybody," the crowd laughed gently. Abigail looked down and pulled something from her pocket. "I loved her though." Abigail raised her hand; her fist concealed some memento of Morgan. Abby turned around and threw the object over the bow into the swells below.

Drucilla stepped up. Her pace was quick. She tore a leather pouch from her neck and held it over the bow. "Fair winds and following seas." Drucilla let the tribute fall into the sea.

Bard caught Kalak looking at him for the first time since Morgan had slipped beneath the waves. Tears burned his eyes as flashes of what happened hours ago flooded his mind. He struggled to find something meaningful to say, but all that came out was, "I-It should have been me."

The monstrous Kalak caught Bard in an embrace, before letting him go.

Drucilla, Mr. Pit, and Abigail had distracted the other crew members by passing around shots of a home-brewed spirit around us.

Kalak held Bard at arm's length. He towered high above him like a grueling demi-god. A solemn look filled Kalak's eyes.

"Promise me one thing, Bard," Kalak's voice echoed with the sincerity of an oath.

"Anything."

"Tell her story. When you tell people about your time on this ship, the megalodon, all of it, don't forget to tell the world who we were, who she was. Else her ghost might come back and finally eat you."

Bard smiled at Kalak's crude attempt at humor. "Of course."

Abigail interrupted at just the right time to hand everyone a shot. Drucilla stood beside her.

Abigail raised her glass. *"To my wild sister of the seas!"* she screamed over the ocean.

Drucilla raised her glass to toast the dead. Her accompanying words were unintelligible to the people around her—a silent prayer in an ancient tongue.

The ship drank and took a moment of silence. Kalak lost his battle and allowed streams of tears to clean streaks through the filth from the battle masking his face. He stood looking out at the waves, holding her garment in his hand. He raised it to his face, imagining it was her he was inhaling her scent one last time. When he opened his eyes, he released her essence to the wind, watching the fabric float on the breeze out to sea.

Kalak stared out at the dark ocean until he was startled by a small hand slipping into his. He looked down to see the little village girl offering her condolences. She was unafraid. He saw the spark, the glimmer of fire in her eyes, the fighting spirit, and it made his heart soften.

"She was amazing," the child said as she squeezed Kalak's fingers.

Kalak's tears dried. A calm washed over him. "Aye."

The ship drank throughout the night. The little girl clung to Kalak's hand, following him everywhere he went. Drucilla tried to pull her away at one point, to reprimand her, but Kalak raised his hand in protest. She saw the look in his eyes and nodded in understanding.

"Tomorrow morning you and I will have a talk about the chain of command, understood?" Drucilla addressed the child. Drucilla knelt down and looked the girl in the eyes.

"She saved my life. I saw her out there. I wanted to meet her so bad," the little girl said to Drucilla. She stole a nervous glance at the morning mass hovering above, and then she turned away from Drucilla completely and detached her hand from Kalak's. Kalak looked down at her. "I want to be like that."

Kalak stared down at her.

"You have to be more hungry than the sharks."

His face was serious. Drucilla feared the child might have offended him. Kalak looked into the little girl's eyes. The little girl did not flinch under his fierce gaze but stared right back without fear.

"Who is she assigned to?" Kalak demanded.

Drucilla stood. "I put her with Vladimir."

Kalak grunted, then looked back down at the child. "Can you fight?"

"Not yet," the little girl answered, "But I am tough."

"You will get hurt all the time. You must learn to laugh at pain."

"I understand."

"If you become a shark fighter, you will die a shark fighter."

"I know."

"You do not want to be mechanic? Safe in the ship."

The little girl smirked, "No, I would go insane."

Drucilla interrupted, "I need her to help Vladimir. She has small hands."

Kalak looked at his captain and met her harsh gaze, "Half and half then. She's not big enough to fight sharks yet. But she'll need to know how to fight one way or another."

Drucilla nodded to herself as she thought about everything that the *Penny Dreadful* needed. She thought of the shark swarm and their defenses. She looked back up at Kalak. He looked apathetic and cruel, but she knew him. He wanted to train the girl. He wished to help her to distract himself. She looked down at the child.

"How old are you?"

"Twelve."

"You're small for twelve."

The girl's face darkened, "That doesn't matter."

A glimmer of approval sparkled in Kalak's eyes.

"If we train you to be a tinkerer and a shark fighter, I need to know you will stay on my ship. I am not going to allow you to distract my workers unless it pays off. Do you understand?"

"Yes," she looked up, "I know how it works. How many years?"

Drucilla thought about it. The child was young enough to learn anything quick. She'd be ready to fight on the open waters by sixteen.

"Four years of training an another eight years of full service. You will be twenty-four before you could leave the *Penny Dreadful.*"

Kalak looked at Drucilla.

The little girl looked to Kalak.

"It is a long time," Kalak said to Drucilla before turning his attention to the questioning child, "This is a good ship though. There are much worse places to end up."

"You cannot change your mind after I brand you. You will be loyal to this ship and the men and women aboard it until your service is over. They will be your family. They will come before everyone else."

"I understand. Yes," the girl did not hesitate. "Brand me now."

Drucilla looked up at Kalak. Kalak crouched down and looked the little girl in the eyes.

"If we do this, and you fail, I will kill you if the sharks don't." Kalak's eyes glossed over with the callous cold that was his usual demeanor.

The girl swallowed and nodded. Kalak stood back up and nodded at Drucilla.

"What is your name," Drucilla asked.

"Artisema."

The initiation of the child was what everyone needed. The booze warmed the bellies. The stories warmed the hearts, and the crew beamed with excitement as Kalak branded the child himself.

The girl eyed the red-hot brand as Kalak approached her. Drucilla and Abigail held her in place by her small biceps. Abigail noticed the unspoken fear in Artisema's big green orbs. She signaled for Kalak to pause, withdrew her belt, and placed it between the girl's teeth to gnaw on.

Anand sulked around the edges of the crowd, glowering at the quick acceptance of the young girl. He watched as they cheered on the girl accepting the brand without a scream escaping from behind the leather strap. The little girl's eyes watered slightly, but no one paid any mind, and the bit of wet dried up as soon as the crew cheered for her.

Mr. Pit stepped from the darkness beside him, startling Anand.

"*You* won't be branded 'til I trust you," Mr. Pit said.

8.

Artisema awoke to Drucilla shaking her. Abigail had set up a small sleeping area for the girl near her rack. Most of the crew already left for work while the child slept soundly through.

"You need to wake up when the crew wakes up," Drucilla was stern, "Get dressed."

The child dressed as quick as she could. Her feet caught on her pant legs as she tried to rush.

"Last night you disobeyed a direct command from your captain. I told you to be quiet and invisible. Everything turned out okay, and I believe you'll be a good distraction for Kalak, but I will not suffer any more defiance to my orders. Is that clear?"

"Yes, ma'am."

"Captain," Drucilla corrected.

"Yes, Captain."

"Good, now follow me to meet Vladimir." Drucilla led the way through the hatch and talked as she walked ahead at a quick pace. "Vladimir needs to be focused. You will obey every single command of his without question or hesitation. When he releases you, you are to report immediately to Kalak above decks. Your hours will be longer than everyone else's because you do not have any experience and need to learn. You will not complain. You will not whine. You will do your job just like everyone else does. I don't care how young you are or how tired you are. I don't care if you are cold or wet or broken or sore. You chose this life, and now you must live it."

Drucilla opened the door to Vladimir's workshop. The tinkerer did not turn from his work when they entered but Drucilla addressed him anyways.

"This is your new assistant. Her name is Artisema. When you finish with her, send her to Kalak."

Vladimir didn't acknowledge Drucilla at all. Drucilla looked down at the girl and then took her leave. The child stood awkwardly waiting for Vladimir to notice her as Drucilla closed the hatch.

As soon as Drucilla arrived on decks, Mr. Pit, Abigail, Kalak, Croatoa, Riddle, and Bard collected around her. Anand lurked a couple of feet behind Mr. Pit.

Mr. Pit turned to him, "What the root you think your doin'? Grab a mop and start swabbin' the decks."

Anand hurried to work, leaving the group to discuss matters amongst themselves.

"I want to pursue the enemy," Drucilla kept her voice down. "I need to know I have full support if I do."

"Aye," Kalak looked at Drucilla.

Croatoa clenched his fists tight, "I'm in."

Everyone nodded in agreement.

"It's settled then. Follow me to my quarters to discuss plans."

"What about him?" Mr. Pit gestured to Anand.

Drucilla looked around. There was plenty of activity all around them. She grabbed the attention of a man splicing line. "Hey, Temit!"

He stopped and stood up, "Yes, Captain."

Drucilla gestured at Anand."Show him how to splice and get him to work!"

"Aye, Captain."

Drucilla led the way to her quarters. She had already spent hours of the morning looking at maps and discretely adjusting their position to pursue the shark swarm. The chart was laid out on the center table. Everyone gathered around, taking the available seats, only Croatoa remained standing, pouring over the map. Drucilla had already sketched a proposed a course of action.

"It looks good to me," Croatoa said, nodding his approval.

"We've been traveling since last night. If we do not find the shark swarm or the Panzer Fish by this point," she jabbed a finger at a small dot on the map, "We will stop and change course for Seattle to reassess the situation, refuel, and unload." No one objected to this plan. Drucilla continued, "Vladimir delivered these to me two days ago. They are plans for more long-range weapons."

Captain Dru laid out sketches of three separate types of weapons. "They will be ready for our arrows next time."

"How much time did they have before we started?"

"Three hours max," Drucilla said.

Kalak smirked, "You didn't waste time changing courses, did ya?"

"I am as driven as your former Captain," Drucilla restacked the weapon blueprints. "I want a 360 watch. The swarm can change their chosen direction for attack faster than we can."

"Aye, aye, Captain," Mr. Pit pushed back his chair and departed to set the watch, "Still can't believe we're chasing a bunch of sharks. You'd think they'd dive so we couldn't follow. Something's not right about them beasts."

"True word Mr. Pit. The rest of you," Drucilla's fierce gaze met her trusted crew members, "Prepare your crews for war."

Croatoa straightened up, "I can take care of the bolts today."

"No," Drucilla looked at the stack of papers, "Report to Vladimir first. He knows what he needs—what we need."

"Alert me the second we see anything, understood?"

"Aye, Aye Captain," Abby replied.

The meeting disbanded. Abigail, Bard and Croatoa went below decks to check in with Vladimir, stopping at the door to Vlad's workshop. A peel of laughter escaped from Vladimir's shop. Anyone who had worked closely with him would swear they had never heard anything so jovial come from there. Nothing except Vladimir screaming ever escaped those doors before now. Bard hesitated before rapping his knuckles against the hatch, remembering all to well his own experiences with Vladimir.

"*Vat is it?*" Vladimir screamed through the door.

Bard pushed the door open to reveal the new girl perched on a step stool at the far end of the room. In front of her was a full machine. When still new on the ship Bard had worked weeks with Vladimir before he had been allowed to help repair anything.

There were two glasses in front of Vlad.

"You gave her alcohol?" Bard asked, slightly shocked, lifting one of the glasses. The girl let out a small burp. A flush was evident in her cheeks. Abigail and Croatoa stepped into the room.

"Vat? My mother—" Vladimir cut through the air with an open palm. "She told me it vas healthy for young lass to know how to drink. I gave her only 'nough to wet her gums. Relax. She vorks hard." Vlad turned away from him and back to his work, "'Sides, I gave you drink too, Bard."

"She's a child!"

"She has job on vale boat. There is no room for child. Now vat do you want?"

Abigail stepped forward, "We are pursuing the shark swarm. Drucilla sent us to see what is needed for you to get those weapons ready for war."

Vladimir turned to the girl, "Have you finished?"

"Ummm," Artesima turned around on the stool. She picked up a screwdriver and tightened a couple of the bolts. Her tiny hands lifted the heavy weapon for inspection. It was the size of a chainsaw with a long protruding barrel. "Yes, I believe so." Her face twisted into an uncertain expression. She pushed it out towards Croatoa and looked at him with knitted brows, "I'd wear fire retardant clothes or have water ready. I don't know how good of a job I did."

Abigail's eyebrows raised, "You let her build weapons?"

"Very talented. Tiny Hands." Vladimir raised his hands in the air and wiggled his fingers for emphasis. "Test flamethrower and report here if she needs to fix it. If it works, ve need fuel prepared. If you find small engines, bring them to me. Maybe ve need a scavenger dive if there is time."

Croatoa held the flamethrower in his hands, looked at the little girl, and laughed. "It's a pleasure to have you on the crew, miss."

The twelve-year-old stood up and gave Croatoa a brief, casual salute, "Pleasure's mine, sir."

As the three of them exited from Vladimir's chambers, Bard practically ran into Anand who was loitering outside of the door with a mop in hand.

"Where's Mr. Pit," Abigail turned on him. "Why are you below decks?"

"P-pit told me to swab the decks."

Abigail straightened up, "I don't want you below decks unattended until you're branded. Lead the way back up."

Mr. Pit was busy trying to save someone's fishing pots. It appeared as if one of the lines snapped. Between him and two other people, they were able to catch the rope and pull the cage from the water.

Bard stood behind Anand, watching Anand closely, absolutely certain that he'd been eavesdropping.

Abigail cut across the deck. "*Mr. Pit!*" she screamed.

"Abby," Mr. Pit dusted his hands off as he walked to meet Abby.

"Did you tell him," she pointed at Anand, "he could go below decks unattended?"

"Root, no!" Mr. Pit's face darkened. His accent thickened as the blood boiled under his skin. He stared suspiciously at the young man.

"Keep a closer eye on him," Abby said, "This is how new fish get thrown overboard even if they don't deserve it." Abigail checked Anand's shoulder as she said this in passing.

"Where are we going to do this at?" Croatoa lifted the flamethrower.

Abby looked around. The skull of the last leviathan lay on the aft end of the ship. It wasn't the most massive skull she'd seen, but it was large enough for Croatoa to stand inside They pushed it next to the railing. Steel plating reinforced the aft and bow but buckets of water were fetched, just in case.

Croatoa slipped on elbow length gloves, an apron, and a welding mask. He aimed the mechanism towards the ocean and pulled the chord to start. The machine made a gurgling sound and stopped anti-climactically. Several doubtful looks were exchanged. Everyone watching seemed to be thinking the same thing—it wasn't going to work.

Croatoa tried pulling the chord again, faster this time. The engine sputtered for a few seconds longer. The effect on the watchers was the same though. Croatoa kept trying.

Abigail finally stepped forward to see if she could help when a massive ball of fire exploded from the front of the weapon and out to sea, causing Croatoa to stumble back, as much from surprise as the force of the explosion.

"Whoa! Wow!" Crotoa lifted his mask. He laughed, "Did you guys see that?"

Abigail stood and smiled. "Take the machine back to Vladimir. Tell him about the unreliable start." She turned to Bard, "I want you to have your boys scour the salvage hold for engine parts as well as oil containers, there's no way the captain will allow us to stop for a dive. I want us to rig a safe station where people can refuel during battle."

Bard nodded and smiled at her and looking casually around to see how visible they were to other crew members, pleased to see that most had departed when Croatoa left with the flamethrower. Slipping a hand around her waist, He traced her warm, smooth, skin with calloused finger tips.

"Abby girl," he murmured close to her ear.

She rolled her eyes, annoyed at being kept from her work, but when she finally looked him in the eyes, she couldn't keep from smiling, "We should catch up to them within hours, Bard."

She bucked, trying to squirm away as Bard kissed her neck. The press of her body against his increased slightly and it wasn't long before she gave in. Her defensive grip grew slack as she lost herself in the sensations pulsating from their embrace. Bard laughed as she finally broke away to catch her breath.

"Such a tease," he said.

"We'll celebrate when we win," she winked before running away over the deck.

9.

The watch called Drucilla at the first signs of human settlement in the waters. They pointed down at large amounts of debris floating on top of the water. Drucilla opened her spyglass and looked out to the horizon.

"There's no sign of the swarm," she said.

"See there though," one of the men pointed out a small stream of black smoke far in the distance. "It's just a wisp, but that's fire."

"Hm," Drucilla closed her glass. "Mr. Pit," her voice rang out across the *Penny Dreadful.*

"Yes, Captain."

"Prepare the archers in case of attack," she stopped for a moment before walking past him to the opposite end of the ship. Over her shoulder, she said, "I think we missed them. Please alert me if there are any new developments."

Drucilla paced the perimeter of the ship with her spyglass. She looked fervently for signs of the hoard, hoping to catch them before they slipped through her grasp again. By the time she reached the watch, keeping eyes on the smoke stream, she could make out a string of boats tethered together.

"It looks like there's maybe twelve of them in total," she said after counting to herself. "They're destroyed. The Panzer Fish were here," she snapped her glass shut. "We're on the right track."

"Everyone prepare to search for survivors. I want two boats to go out to the settlement while the rest of us protect the ship. Keep a weather eye for any remaining cultists and take note what direction they're are moving in."

The ship bustled with action. Within moments two lancer vessels were rowing over the swells to the destroyed chain of ships. Drucilla climbed to the crow's nest to see if she could catch a glimpse of anything. She thought she spotted a dark mass briefly curving out of sight in the distance, but it was impossible to tell. It was too late to retract her boats and pursue it. She decided to wait for the return reports of her men.

It was not long before the small units returned to the *Penny Dreadful*. Drucilla was not surprised to find them come back with only a couple items between them. Kalak's face was red from seeing the wreckage. He passed Drucilla without acknowledgment.

"Well," Drucilla said.

Mr. Pit boarded and stepped aside to talk to the captain.

"It's the Panzer Fish. We only found one survivor, but between us I think death would have been a mercy for her," Mr. Pit grabbed Drucilla's arm. "They're headed for Seattle, Captain. I suppose they're a bit loose at the tongue when they've already won."

Drucilla didn't even blink. "Make the necessary preparations. Meet in my quarters as soon as we are underway."

"Aye."

Seattle was their home port. Drucilla's father, Captain Raj, lost his life defending Seattle from the mutated megalodon the Panzer Fish worshipped. They needed to get there as fast as they could. She needed to try and beat the swarm to Seattle if possible and warn the inhabitants. Drucilla glanced out at the dilapidated wreckage.

As Mr. Pit turned to leave, Drucilla caught him. "Did the survivor say how many of them there were?"

Mr. Pit stopped and turned to face Drucilla. She saw it in his eyes. He did not want to worry her with the knowledge. Drucilla sighed.

"How many more?"

"A full army, Cap'n. The cult has grown more than we thought. They're gonna hit Seattle with everything they've got. Here's the thing Captain, they want revenge for what we did to Kaiku, and since we sailed from Seattle, that's where they're going. Panzers left her alive as a message, for us. We'd best sail with care."

Drucilla closed her eyes for a moment and tried to collect herself. There was no time to waste. "Make sure Vladimir has all the help we can afford for amassing weapons, cannibalize every scrap of unused material on this ship. When we arrive in Seattle's ports, I want to be prepared with all of our new equipment. Make sure he reports to my quarters as well."

"Aye." Mr. Pit gave Drucilla a curt nod before turning to organize the ship.

Hardly any time passed before Abigail, Croatoa, Riddle, Mr. Pit, Kalak, Vladimir, and Bard crowded Drucilla's captain's quarters to discuss their plan of attack.

Above decks, Anand worked alongside the other men, preparing for the upcoming battle. Vladimir left Artisema in charge of delegating work in his absence. She was to march the decks inspecting bolts for the archers, the catapults, flamethrowers, and keeping everyone on task until everyone returned from the meeting.

Artisema and Anand had hardly interacted since they boarded the ship. She didn't recognize him at first. He kept his back turned as he conversed with a group of eight or nine men, some of them survivors from the village who had also found a place on board but had not yet earned their brands. Initially, Artisema was under the impression they were working together, but as she approached them she silenced her approach to hear what they had to say.

"It's bullshit, you know," Anand's was a hoarse whisper. "I didn't leave the fuckin' village to die in a war against the Panzer Fish, nobody has been able to stand up to them before, why would now be any different? I came to be a whaler, you know?"

The men muttered in agreement.

"We have to do something," Anand continued.

"Do what?" Artisema stepped out of the shadows concealing her from the men's vision. Anand startled at her presence behind him.

He stood up. "Artisema, join us. We almost died back there in the village. It's not fair they've made you do slave labor, and now they also want you to die for a city leagues away that you have no loyalty to."

Artisema studied Anand's features as he towered over her. She didn't know what else to do, so she said, "If you are not going to help make weapons, will you please do something else, so I don't get in trouble?" She glanced at the men. They whispered to one another. Some of them scowled at her.

"Of course," Anand gave her a weak smile, "Hey, this is our little secret, okay. Just remember, whatever happens, I'm like a brother to you now. We came from the same village and everything."

Artisema held her tongue. She couldn't remember seeing him once in her village before that day. "Just do some work, okay?"

Artisema, not wanting to draw any more attention from the gang of rough whalers eyeing her, turned at that point and busied herself with the job assigned to her. It was not long before Vladimir came above decks. The others were still convened down below.

"Vat did I miss?" He asked.

Artisema opened her mouth to speak. In her peripheral, she noticed the gaze of Anand and the other would be whalers and sailors. She smiled at Vladimir, "Nothing. It's all coming along as planned."

"Very good. You may take day off to vork with Kalak or rest. Tomorrow I have 'nother long day for you."

She nodded. "Are you sure?"

"Yes, yes, be gone, little girl. You've done enough today."

Artisema glanced at Anand as she left. He heard everything and smiled at her as if they were compatriots. He lifted a finger to his lips, gesturing for the conspiracy to keep silent. Artisema did not like what she'd heard.

She quickened her pace past and was about to report below deck when she noticed one of the men trailing behind her. He kept a hundred feet behind her, but he made it clear that Anand's party was keeping a close eye on her.

The little girl found a spot to wait for Kalak. She stared out at sea trying to decide who she would tell and how she would get the privacy to do it.

10.

Drucilla hid away in her personal quarters as her crew worked to prepare the ship for battle. She needed to be sharp. There was no telling how many cultists they would find. They could have had a party waiting nearby with reinforcements. Drucilla opened book after book on shark behavior. Over the last 80 years, many accomplished whalers had written tomes of their successes and failures, and her father has always been something of a reader.

In her father's private collection, she found a worn copy of, *"Kaiku and other Great Beasts: An Account of Modern Mythology."* It was handwritten. Each letter carved into the page with great care. The narrator admitted to being a part of the Panzer Fish. Most of the information Drucilla already knew. They worshiped the giant shark the *Penny Dreadful* had taken down the year before, believing the sharks sought to destroy the human race as punishment for causing the Great Melt, and they had no regard for human life whatsoever.

What Drucilla really wanted to know was what a particular symbol meant. Drucilla remembered seeing it on the megalodon right before it disappeared with her father in tow. She would never forget the marking, had never seen anything like it before. She had watched the whole battle with her spyglass and noticed it on the sharks in the shark swarm. Not one shark attacked a Panzer Fish. They had worked as a team and had left as a unit.

Halfway through the musty, old book she found it, a crude drawing of the mark she was looking for. It was in a chapter titled, *Holy Symbols*, but that was it. The author wrote all of the other information in a strange language.

An urgent knock pounded on her door. Drucilla slammed the book closed and looked out the porthole. It was night. Drucilla answered the door to find the small village child out of breath.

"Artisema, what—" Drucilla was interrupted by the little girl raising her hands up as she gulped for air.

"Please, Captain, I need to tell you something."

"Where is Kalak? Why are you not with Vladimir or Kalak?"

"It's important," the girl insisted, pushing past Drucilla into the room and closing the door behind her.

"I overheard Anand talking to some of the other crew members and a few survivors from Blue Stone. I wanted to tell you earlier, but they were watching me. He plans on doing something, I don't know what," her eyes welled as if she was about to cry, "Please, don't kick me off the ship."

Drucilla pursed her lips. "How did you get away from Kalak and Vladimir?"

"They think I'm still sleeping."

"Did anyone see you come to me?"

"I-I don't know. I don't think so."

"Good," Drucilla paused for a moment to think. "I need you to find Croatoa and tell him to prepare his diving gear. Don't let anyone see or hear you."

The little girl turned to leave. Drucilla grabbed her arm suddenly, "Keep your teeth apart during war."

The little girl looked up at Drucilla. It took her a moment to realize she meant in case something impacted the ship. Artisema smiled at the concern before slipping away to find Croatoa. Drucilla had enough time to stow her papers when an explosion rippled through the *Penny Dreadful*.

"Damn it."

Drucilla ran with all of her might to the source of the sound. There were already men inside of the flooding compartments below decks.

"Seal the doors! Seal off the damage before we sink!" she shouted. The men seemed to take their time sealing off the door. "I swear, if you don't move your asses, I will seal you inside!" The men quickened their pace.

"Help me, damn it!" She screamed at them, as the pressure of the water flooding in threatened to prevent her from sealing the compartment off. Mr. Pit arrived just in time to help Drucilla seal the door.

"Mr. Pit, where is your ward?"

Mr. Pit looked angry, disgusted and chagrined at the same time. "He's escaped," he stated.

Drucilla screamed at the top of her lungs. *"Find him!"*

Abigail, Artisema, Croatoa, and Bard showed up at nearly the same time. People fled the scene as they approached until Drucilla was the only one left. Croatoa wore his diving bell and suit. Artisema told him to gear up moments before the explosion hit. It became clear why Drucilla wanted him to suit up when the second the blast rattled through the ship.

Drucilla's face burned with fury, *"Croatoa, get out there with a crew and start fixing the ship!"*

"Yes, Captain!"

"Abigail. Bard. Get those fuckers. You saw them. I won't be surprised if they're wreaking havoc on my ship. You saw 'em right?"

Bard nodded. Abigail turned on her heel and followed him down the corridor.

"Artisema, find Kalak, describe the men to him. Then go straight to Vladimir. Do everything he says as fast and good as you possibly can, understand?" Drucilla crouched down and held Artisema's gaze with her own.

The young girl gave a curt nod. She'd pulled her chin length hair into two small nubs of pigtails at the back of her head that bobbed with the motion and ran off in search of Kalak.

Drucilla took a deep breath. She felt the thick bulkheads separating her from the ocean. Drucilla went through all of the surrounding compartments, ensuring no one remained inside. She sealed all the chambers off on that floor to protect the ship in case the damage and pressure of the water caused one of the bulkheads to cave in. When the lower decks were adequately sealed off, she went topside of the *Penny Dreadful*.

Her crew was in chaos. Mr. Pit, Kalak, Bard, and Abigail cornered three armed men, one of whom was Anand. Although trapped, they still attempted to fight their way through. Abigail's arm sported a bloody slash. Riddle stood with her gun mount guarding the four men already apprehended and tied up. She kept her weapon trained on them.

"Mr. Pit, detain those men immediately by any means!"

Mr. Pit looked at Anand and smiled, calling over his shoulder, "Ya, hear that, mates? By any means," He raised his war hammer and with one swift blow took out Anand's knees.

The leader of the mutiny screamed and fell, writhing, to the ground. He looked up at Drucilla as she studied him with cold hatred.

Mr. Pit kicked him.

Anand screamed and then spit blood on the deck, "You'll never beat them! They fight with the power of Kaiku!"

Drucilla's eyes narrowed into slits. "My father killed *Kaiku*," She sneered.

Drucilla looked at the men. "Execute them." Louder, she announced to the rest of the crew, "Anyone else who doesn't want to fight can leave the ship when we arrive at Seattle's port. Until then, death will be the penalty for mutiny and desertion. As if it would ever be anything less."

One of the crew members stepped forth, "We stand next to you Captain. That's our home too. You look and them lads is either from Blue Stone or part of the new crew we picked up in the Sargasso."

Drucilla lifted her head a little higher and smiled faintly as the assembled crew nodded and commented among themselves. "I'm glad to hear that." She turned her head to address Riddle. "We have no time to waste. Riddle, please --" Drucilla was cut off as eight rounds were instantly fired from the young woman's arm into the skulls of the rebels.

After the ringing ceased in Dru's ears, she continued, "Clean up this mess now. Mr. Pit and Kalak, if he really was one of the Panzers there may will be sharks in the water soon. We don't know what kind of communication Anand might have had with them. I need you and the sharkers in the water. Everyone else is on a triple watch, all divers with Croatoa below decks on repairing the ship. Am I understood?"

11.

The work crews had only been at it for an hour or so when Drucilla withdrew her spyglass from her belt. On the horizon, approaching fast, a splinter group from the shark swarm appeared, silhouetted against the silvery moonlight.

"To arms!" Drucilla shouted to each component of her crew, "Bard. Abigail. Lancing boats, now! Get a picket line and blunt the charge. Croatoa and his men need protection while they're repairing the hull. Kalak and Mr. Pit keep a weather eye and, *get those sharks!"*

The ship erupted into action to save the *Penny Dreadful* from a grisly fate. The boats were ready and deployed within moments. Fog rolled over the calm waves, licking the sides of the vessels. The oars whipped through the ominous silence reaching over the dark waters. Only a few cultists were riding with the splinter swarm. The sound of their jet skis was the first sign the *Penny Dreadful's* welcoming party had of their approach as the fog rolled over them.

Bard signaled to Abigail, telling her he could hear the cultists in the thick fog. The oar men stayed their movement in hopes of surprising the oncoming attack. The crew strained for sounds of sharks cutting through the water around them: for the jet skis to roar within striking distance. They held their breath as they hid beneath the thickening veil of fog.

Kalak and Mr. Pit took longer to reach the lancing vessels' position. They didn't need a command. Their engines silenced upon arrival. Unfortunately, as the party strained in the renewed silence, the Panzer Fish were unheard. They must have taken note of Kalak and Mr. Pit's loud approach. The crew of the *Penny Dreadful* tightened their grips around their weapons. Their oars were traded for lances. The boards groaned, soft into the breeze, under the shifting weight of men and women preparing for action.

Kalak's jet ski drifted out starboard from the formation. He found himself in a thick plume of white and grey mist. Under a break through the clouds and fog, a shaft of moonlight fell upon a

Panzer Fish, his bone armor reflecting white under the night's light. Kalak took the utmost care in timing his attack. The cultist eyed the nearby fog with suspicion. He peered right at Kalak, without seeing him, unknowing of what waited for him.

He inched closer and closer to Kalak. In the same moment, Kalak's grin appeared through the misty veil, the revving of his chainsaw broking the silence pressing in around them. Within seconds, Kalak's jet ski lurched forward, and the teeth of his weapon ate through the leather protecting the Panzer's guts, blood spraying into the mist. The lancers took Kalak's cue and attacked the infiltrating targets.

All around, sharks exploded to the surface as lances bored into their thick, armored flesh. The few Panzer Fish still stalking through the fog turned on the boats. Four of them in total assaulted Abigail and Bard's units. One jet ski skipped towards Bard, exploding from a burst of cold, sea vapor. The gruesome face of his attacker flickered in and out of the moonlight as he raised a broadsword to strike. Bard released his harpoon on instinct, his throw perfect, and the Panzer's body tumbled off the saddle and the jet ski spun out of control into the waves.

Abigail leaped from the bow of her boat landing a solid punch into the face of another cultist, though he managed to maintain an unsteady grip on the steering of the jet ski. Abigail grabbed onto the front of his bone ornamented vest, her other hand gripping the hilt of a long curved blade. She slashed the knife across the cultist's throat, turning her head up to avoid the fountain of spraying blood. She threw the corpse, gulping for its last bloody breaths, to the waves and commandeered his jet ski.

All Croatoa needed to do was concentrate on repairing the hull while the others focused on protection. The visibility was low. Aside from the massive amounts of blood fading like clouds around them, the water was dark and grainy.

The crew above managed to block the sharks and Panzer Fish from getting too close to the ship. Down below the dark waters,

Croatoa and the men worked in low visibility on the *Penny Dreadful*. Even with the torches lighting the area around them, the water was still grainy and difficult to see through. The watertight lanterns would only stay lit for about a minute before the candle flames burned up all the oxygen and they went dark again, and even with the steady stream of re-lit lanterns the work was slow going.

"Come on!" Croatoa rushed himself, *"Come on!"*

He heard a gargled, underwater scream, and turned his head just in time to witness one of his men vanish suddenly, dragged down by some unknown force, into the black abyss below. The other divers, not needed to help Croatoa anymore, armed themselves with knives and short stabbing spears to protect him and the last bit of work required to secure the hull's patch. The crew fighting the sharks above were unaware of the new threat down below. Croatoa looked at them, looked down below, and then continued the last bits of the job. The whale oil fueling his welding torch burned an ugly orange in the murky night sea, and yet in its light he could see far more of the conflict around him than he cared too. He tried to focus on the bright blue and searing red in front of him, pushing the mysterious sea demon from his mind.

Croatoa saw the dark shadows of the creature rise in the light dancing on the hull of the ship. He reminded himself he couldn't get him and his men away until he finished the job. One minute, that's all he needed. He knew his men battled whatever filled the water behind him even though he could hear nothing. Finished at last, Croatoa turned to join the fight. An enormous sea serpent, one of the nocturnal nightmares that made night whaling a deadly prospect indeed, drawn to the surface by the light, the gore, and the violence.

Croatoa blasted the serpent's belly with the bright blue flame of his blow torch. The other divers had given it a few gashes on its thick hide, despite some of them paying with their lives in exchange for the blows, and thankfully Croatoa's torch attack was finally enough to get a shriek from the creature as it broke the surface of the water with its head.

On the surface, Kalak and Mr. Pit were focusing their eyes away from the hull of the ship. They were so focused on the sharks that Kalak nearly fell from his jet ski when the head of the sea serpent, a dark blue scaly column, rose screaming from the waters high above them. Kalak was not a man taken off guard easily and his body acted automatically to this unexpected turn of events and he shoved the chainsaw right through the trunk of the creature, not registering the potential dangers this could raise.

The sea serpent let out a cry that would haunt every man and woman who heard it till their dying day. The sound blasted through the air, clawing at the ears of each man and woman on and surrounding the *Penny Dreadful.*

Drucilla looked over the railing of the ship and gaped at the slender head and black beady eyes of the massive creature. "*ARCHERS!*" She screamed.

The fastest archers aimed for the eyes and face of the creature. Kalak tried his best to saw his way through the thick flesh of the beast. His chainsaw was only a third of the way through and hard pressed to maintain his footing as the beast thrashed against the rotating blades. Mr. Pit aided Croatoa and the other divers to safety on the ship.

Finally, one of Riddle's projectiles lodged itself in the brain of the enormous monster. The muscles in the body relaxed, the head swaying. Kalak looked up to see the thick, elongated body falling rapidly to the ocean. He ripped his chainsaw away and leaped into the sea's waves as the body crashed down on his jet ski, where he stood seconds before.

The bulk of the shark swarm had fled with the appearance of the massive sea creature. The Panzer Fish were dead or had fled back into the fog as it receded, and the few sharks too frenzied to flee had been picked off by the skilled crew of the *Penny Dreadful.*

Dawn broke over the waterline as the exhausted crew gathered themselves. The orange and reds of the coming sunrise mingled with the bloody water and it was impossible to tell where one stopped and the other began.

A costly victory, but one that saw the ship and her crew greet the dawn still afloat.

12.

The *Penny Dreadful's* spirits renewed with the conquering of the splinter group, the men and women roaring with excitement at having surviving the harrowing night. The crew welcomed Croatoa aboard as a hero.

Croatoa was the only diver to survive. The other two had been torn to pieces right next to him. Exhausted and angry from the stress and the loss of his men, Croatoa spit on the bleeding corpse of Anand as he passed by and walked straight below decks to his berthing.

The sounds of music and dancing echoed from above decks. Bard showed Kalak a bottle of homebrew hidden under his jacket and gestured for him to sneak away behind Croatoa. They had just enough time to remove their boots before Drucilla appeared at the entrance. She stood with the poise of a commander in the threshold where she hesitated. Kalak, Croatoa, and Bard looked up at her, waiting for a command.

Drucilla's shrewd eyes saw they were exhausted. She exhaled, and her body relaxed against the bulkhead. Captain Dru walked across the room and ran her finger along the railing of her old rack. She let her body flop back, breaking her bearing, and allowing herself to relax away from the eyes of the rest of the crew. Bard smiled and locked the door to avoid anyone seeing the captain taking a break from fixing the ship, planning attacks, and just being captain.

"You were all amazing out there," Drucilla whispered.

Croatoa was silent. Drucilla looked at him. Even exhausted, Croatoa was known for always keeping a sunny disposition. He grew up in the crabbing communities of Seattle which was a rough place to learn about life. Croatoa was not new to death and the harsh conditions out at sea. Seeing him solemn concerned Drucilla. If this attack had sapped his default joy, she couldn't imagine how the rest of the crew were coping.

"Croatoa," Captain Dru said.

He held his head in his hands. "What? A lancer and two sharkers lost at Blue Stone? Three men drowned belowdecks from the explosion? Eight turned mutineer? Sarver and Hagil just died right next to me," he looked up at Drucilla, "We are now but a skeleton crew Captain."

Drucilla sat up. Bard and Kalak tried to avoid eye contact but listened intensely.

"Do we stand a chance if we find the fight we're looking for?" His voiced peaked in a manic moment.

"There's no guarantee, but if anyone is going to stop them, it'll be us. There aren't many choices. If we don't fight, they will slaughter us. If we do fight, they still might slaughter us."

Croatoa pawed his chest as if he was experiencing pain. Kalak stood up. A grim expression concealed his emotions. The scars and lines marking his skin looked carved from stone.

"They killed Morgan."

Croatoa calmed a moment upon seeing Kalak's eyes. He softened. "That's not what I meant, Kalak. I want to make them pay too, but we need to come up with a serious plan. They're going to beat us to Seattle, and when we sail against them we'll be at half strength."

"We'll have help there," Bard broke in. The cork popped from the homebrew and fizzled in the silent pause. Bard ignored Drucilla's glance and took a pull from the bottle before passing it to Croatoa.

Croatoa held the bottle for a moment. "Yeah, still though. They haven't prepared as we have. You saw them try to fight Kaiku." He took a swig and handed the bottle to Kalak. "Dru, we have to do something and," he gestured his hands, "And you can't be seen relaxing. I'm sorry, but we've already had one mutiny—"

Drucilla jumped to her feet in defense, "That was led by a cultist. You know that."

"Yeah, but a few of our men still joined." Croatoa sighed. "It doesn't matter if they were the new blood from Sargasso. I know you're doing your best, but I'm telling you, there will be more unrest and deserters if they think you don't tighten up the ship. Trust me. Perception is everything."

Drucilla sat down. He was right. She knew it. She looked at Bard. He stood up and locked the door, nodding in agreement with Croatoa.   "It's   true."

"Are you guys telling me to leave?"

"Fuck, no," Kalak said and passed her the bottle.

"We're saying relax here behind closed doors, but when you leave that door, you better look like we've been discussing plans the whole night while everyone else gets shitty. In fact, you should probably address the crew tonight. We need Vladimir working night and day. That small child you brought on board," Croatoa pointed to the door, "She better be ready in the event that the Panzers take the ship. Us they'll kill right away, but you know what they do to girls like her."

Drucilla knew.

There was a moment of silence. The bottle passed around while everyone contemplated the last few weeks and what approached them.

After a few more moments, Bard pulled his banjo from his rack and strummed a few soothing chords. "We have to have killed off quite a few of them already."

"Yeah, but we don't know how many of them will meet us in Seattle," Croatoa grumbled, "There have been stories about them for years, and we've heard tell that there have been sightings of those altar bouys from here to the edge of the world."

"Look, Croatoa, we are all tired." Bard replied. "We need rest. We still have time before we reach Seattle. Our long-range weapons get better by the day. Vladimir has worked around the clock to ensure we have enough ammo. He's even developed an underwater ordinance for you and your diving crews. I mean, sorry, when you train up a new dive crew."

"Do we have a plan for when we get there?" Croatoa asked.

Dru shook her head, "It's hard to tell. I've thought of quite a few possibilities, but it will depend on what we find there. I'm assuming we won't need the lancing vessels. There will be people on Seattle's docks and separating our men sounds dangerous."

"Aye," Bard agreed.

Dru continued, "I think we need an underwater team, they'll expect us to fight from boats and the ship, just like Blue Stone. I say we treat it like crab season, and as we rain fire on them from above on our ship, we put killers in the water beneath them."

Croatoa sighed and fell back into his rack. He pressed the palms of his hands into his eyes. "As soon as this is over, I am spending at least a week in a brothel at the *Penny Dreadful's* expense."

The room shook with sudden laughter. Drucilla took one more drink before standing up and reclaiming the demeanor of a cold-blooded whaling captain. "Get some rest. The next weeks are going to be hard. Croatoa, I know today was horrid. I can't imagine what it was like patching the hull with everything going on around you, but you need to stay strong until this is over."

Bard opened the door slightly as she delivered the rest of the commands. The tone of her voice shifted as she became aware of people in the passageways. "You will check and repair all of the diving gear. I want you to select men for underwater battle and run training exercises with them daily, understood?"

Croatoa gave a weak smile, "Aye-aye, Captain."

"Kalak, every single sharker left is going to have to be ready to rack the kill count of three. Bard during the day you will run support. First priority is Vladimir, second priority is Croatoa, third priority is Mr. Pit, and then on down the chain. I also want you to work harder on up keeping morale with that damn banjo of yours. Good evening gentlemen."

Drucilla exited through the hatch. The three of them could hear her holler down the passageways for the rest of the crew to wind down and prepare for the next day.

Within the next hour, everyone was sleeping soundly except Croatoa who stared blankly overhead. The day replayed in his head. It took him hours to push the thoughts and fears from his brain until his mind finally fixated on the image of Morgan.

And then Sarver. Hagil. Rex. Jameson. Valeria. Damos. Captain Raj. So many others.

There was no growing old in this business.

13.

When Croatoa awoke, his berthing was empty except for the child. He did not stir from his rack and observed her for a moment. She sat on Abigail's bed cradling a hunk of metal that appeared to be a small engine of sorts. Artisema's tiny hands worked diligently with a screwdriver trying to fix whatever it was in her little arms.

"Have you always been mechanical?"

Croatoa's voice startled her. She nearly dropped the machine.

"My dad was an engineer, before the Mega," she looked back down at the greasy part in her lap, "One of the best. I'd help him a lot. I like doing this with Vladimir."

"Huh," Croatoa looked up at the ceiling for a moment before letting out a long sigh and swinging his legs over the side of the bed.

Artisema was a scrawny little girl. Croatoa's voice was flat and apathetic, "Do you know what is coming?"

"Mhm. War."

"And do you know what happens to little girls in war?"

Artisema looked at Croatoa. Her face was blank. She set the engine down on the floor and smeared the grease around on her hands. "Yes, I do."

Croatoa half laughed. "You're just a child. You shouldn't be here."

"But I am, and I don't think you should worry about me."

"Oh yeah? If we fail in Seattle," Croatoa met her green eyes and let her have the unvarnished truth. "They will take turns raping you. Then the captain. Then Abigail. Then they will dismember you and then throw the pieces of your corpse to their pet sharks and continue on with their day."

Artisema's face blanched white then flushed red. "I know," she looked down at her hands, running her nails along her finger beds to remove some of the black grime, "The attack at my village wasn't the first time. I've seen them before."

Croatoa raised his eyebrows. "Yeah?"

"Yeah, I've got to go back to Vladimir. You should probably get to work. Captain told everyone not to disturb you this morning, but they're waiting for you, y'know?"

Artisema stood up to leave. She buckled slightly under the weight of the engine.

"Hey," Croatoa piped up just as she was about to leave, "I'm sorry."

Artisema shifted her weight, "It's okay. You need to get it together though. I don't need scaring, I know what is at stake. At least you have a chance to save your home." She disappeared through the passageway, leaving Croatoa to himself and his thoughts.

The ship was in full swing when Croatoa appeared above decks. Every man and woman greeted him personally as he passed.

"Good morning!"

"Congratulations!"

"Here comes the hero of the day!"

"That serpent, huh?"

Croatoa nodded through it. Artisema's words rolled over and over in his mind. She was right. This was not the time to feel sorry. This was the time to fight tooth and nail for his home—for Seattle. He spent a couple of moments clearing his head as he watched the grey ocean waters pass by the ship. Drucilla passed by him. He hooked his hand around her elbow.

"Hey, can I talk to you?" She looked down at his hand on her arm. He released it.

"Yeah," she said, "Meet me in my quarters in twenty minutes."

Drucilla disappeared. Croatoa decided to relax until she was ready, contemplating which men he would need for conducting the underwater attack. He knew the city's structure better than anyone. He knew what needed to be protected. His mind rolled with the dangers of the tight spaces. All of them were businesses and apartments drowned by the Great Melt. Twenty minutes slipped by. Croatoa waited a little extra time and enjoyed the calm of the gray waves before turning to meet with Drucilla.

Drucilla sat alone in her chambers. Various planning materials cluttered her table. Croatoa slumped in one of the chairs surrounding the hodge-podge of maps and papers and equipment sketches.

"Who is free to be a part of my team?" Croatoa asked.

Drucilla did not look up as he mentioned this. She continued to diligently scribble in a leather bound book stacked upon the layers of paper coating her desk. She took her time before answering.

"Who do you want?" She asked.

"Abigail and Bard for sure."

"No go for Abigail. I have her on deck with me running the archers."

Croatoa nodded, "Who do you have available?"

Drucilla pulled a piece of parchment with eight names on it.

"Most of these people have never even hunted crab," Croatoa scoffed.

"They are some of our strongest men."

"In what way?"

Drucilla set down her pen and looked up at him, "Look, our numbers have dwindled. That is who you have to choose from. Take all of them or none. I'll give you Bard, but these men are who you have to choose from."

Croatoa took the piece of parchment and curled it in his hand. The men would work, but he wanted experts down there with him. Croatoa left without another word, thinking about how he would manage to keep these men alive.

The lockers with the diving gear were below decks and on the aft end of the ship. There were ten suits in total, but before even looking, Croatoa knew most of them were damaged. He looked at the parchment again. Sailor Dave and Chimp were great men above the waters, but Croatoa had no idea what they would be like beneath the ocean in that environment. They were his best bet to start with, aside from Bard.

Croatoa left the diving lockers in search of the two men. He found Sailor servicing makeshift catapults. He stood half a foot taller than Croatoa. The majority of his skin was marked with dark tattoos depicting his trials upon the ocean.

"Hey, Sailor Dave," Dave perked up at the sound of Croatoa's voice. "I need a team to work with me when we get to Seattle. We'll be diving while the crew tackles the sharks overhead, and makes sure the swarm doesn't damage Seattle's structures and sink what dry land is left. This is the list Drucilla gave me for possible men. If you work with me, I'll train you, but I'm not sure which of these other men will be of help to us."

Sailor Dave took the list and thought a moment before handing it back.

"I'm not a diver mate, just a sailor" he said, and then added without a hint of humor, "It's in the name."

Croatoa sighed at this response. Dave was a simple man, and much could be lost on him if one did not word things the right way.

"I'll do what I can though, sir."

Croatoa looked up, "Really?"

"Yeah, after everything you've done for the *Penny Dreadful*, I'd follow you anywhere. These men won't like the idea of diving. I know them, though. I can help get them on board."

"Thank you," Croatoa said, "Please, take your time getting them. Meet me in the diving lockers with whomever you can get, and we'll start preparations."

"Aye."

Sailor took the list, and Croatoa departed back to the lockers. He laid out all of the suits and started the process of checking the neoprene for wear and tear. All the sealant available fit into the palm of his hand.

He prayed it would be enough to at least have eight men on his team.

14.

A grueling few days of hard labor and endless training later, the crew on the *Penny Dreadful* watched as dark plumes of smoke rose from the horizon before them. The thick, black smoke of burning whale oil clouded the air with the shroud of war, darkened all the more by Seattle's notoriously frequent bouts of low clouds and falling mist. As Drucilla stood at the helm of her ship and watched through the cracked glass of the wheelhouse an explosion sounded in the distance and one of Seattle's buildings fell into the ocean.

On deck, Mr. Pit commanded for the divers to prepare themselves. They were to take a small lancing boat and sneak into Seattle while the *Penny Dreadful* distracted the bulk of the marauders. Two whaling vessels floated near Seattle's shores as the masts of a third could be seen sinking into the bay. They discharged everything they had at the swarm of cultists and sharks attacking the settlements and vessels.

Croatoa took a deep breath as he looked at the chaos. Nine men, including Bard and himself, climbed down into a lancing boat. Each of them were armed with whatever weapons felt most comfortable. Confidence in their abilities was just as important as their weapons at this point.

The lancing boat bobbed silently in the black shadows of the *Penny Dreadful*. Only two rowers worked for the sake of invisibility. Croatoa and Bard took on the responsibility for keeping cover, gently pulling their oars through the water. Every rower kept their eyes peeled—shifting around the horizon for threats while maintaining their focus on the heat of the action collecting in the distance on Seattle's main port.

The movement was slow and steady. Croatoa could see the best way to enter the city. He trusted the others to keep watch more than he should as he set his eyes upon the small entrance in the distance. The cloud cover was thick, the waves were dark. So dark that save for the waves licking at the sides of the boat, it would seem as if they floated rather than sailed.

The sound of screams bounced off the waves along with the odor of sulfur from Seattle's small armory issuing cannon fire. The waves would light up in a magnetic, warm explosion of red and pink and orange, revealing the dorsal fins projecting from the water and nearly giving their position away in the brief flashes of light.

A third flash blasted across the waters. When it did, they were surprised to find three sharks circling the boat. The sharks were just as surprised, and in that moment of jarring awareness, everyone attacked—man and shark alike. Sailor Dave was the first to strike. Startled by the sudden appearance of a long, spotted beast lurching up and snapping it's jaws, he impaled it with his spear right down the throat of the creature, feeling its teeth scrape along his forearm leaving long bleeding gashes to attract more predators.

There were two to three weapons for each person. Everyone had either a harpoon or a spear on top of their weapon of choice for beneath the sea. Although the sharks tore at them and fought as hard as they could, the team was well-trained and scared enough to fight for their lives in the most brutal manner. Blood exploded from bludgeons when the spears were not enough to massacre the attacking creatures.

The bodies of the sharks sank, but the blood clouded out all around them.

"We need to move fast," Croatoa said.

Their efforts doubled. Luck was on their side because the Seattle's cannons had gone silent, whether the gunners had been slain or the armor had run out of dry powder or shot, they could only guess. They could still hear the rage of the battle, but no longer was the small party placed on lighted display.

It took us at least thirty minutes to get to the edge of the city. Croatoa directed them down a small channel forged between floating atolls decorating the last bits of buildings penetrating the seascape. The little boat drifted down the silent corridor, set apart from the main rage of the battle, the structures muting the majority of the sounds.

"Dock over here," Croatoa commanded.

Bard stepped onto the docks and lashed a rope around one of the cleats. The men did not speak as they prepared for what came next, taking stock of their ordinance, securing it to themselves and ensuring everything would stay put as they traveled down to the fathoms below.

Each of them had light sticks, but none of them were to be used until they were cast into complete and utter darkness. Dawn would penetrate the waters soon enough and the sharks would know they were there. Until then, they hoped to maintain the element of surprise as they descended to the depths below.

Below the waters were the remains of pre-apocalyptic Seattle. Down below were apartment buildings re-inhabited by mutated fish, giant crabs, and scummy water. Far, far, below the surface, the small team descended, armed and ready to defend the structures holding up Seattle. Croatoa knew what needed to be defended the most. Pike's Place was a top priority, as well as the constable's office, and the hospital.

The waters were dark and murky, the underwater world consisted of silhouettes. There were vague outlines penetrating the dark abyss. They drifted slowly down, adjusting to the pressure changes. Eyes remained peeled open, constantly looking around for threats. The battle in the distance was dulled by the water pressing in upon them. Only the muffled blasts from the war raging above penetrated the waters as muted, distant booming.

There was a sort of peace in the waters as they made their way towards the battlefield. Although everyone was alert, no sharks were hidden in the alleys or shops, no fish or crab or human. This led to a false security. Yes, they were prepared, their minds trained on their inevitable fate. In the backs of their minds everyone knew that at any moment they could be attacked, but muscles still softened from the relief of the silence surrounding them.

The cityscape looked beautiful shaded beneath the green and blue haze of the ocean as they moved down the ancient alley ways. Rusted steel carcasses scattered about obstructing their movements but also concealed at the same time. Hearts pounded in anticipation even though there was still quite some time until they reached the edges of the battlefield.

Croatoa led the procession towards the center of the city. In his mind, the highest priority was the hospital despite the counseling of Drucilla. He knew the truth about battle. He knew the truth of the people growing up like him. The hospital was the most important institution. The banks could burn. Even Pike's Place could be rebuilt. Trade could go on without a structure, but the people needed a hospital.

16.

Mr. Pit orchestrated the archers aboard the deck of the *Penny Dreadful* as the whaleship plunged into the thick of the fighting, sailing right into the teeth of the bay. All around them the jaws of hungry sharks snapped in the waters around them as the Panzer Fish tried to board.

"Archers! Those bastards are your top priority! Don't let them board the ship!"

Riddle attached a machine to the mechanical mount where her arm used to be. She stood at the railing of the *Penny Dreadful*, looking down at the men crawling up the sides of the vessel. They lodged their feet and hands in the cracks between the overlapping metal plates. Four of them clambered up the portion of the ship she was responsible for.

Riddle's long red hair whipped in the sea breeze. She could see the twinkling of knives caught between the teeth of the Panzer Fish. The wind shifted and the black smoke moved so that the sun peeked out ever so slightly. This was her chance. Attached to her arm was a device for launching tiny harpoons. They were too small for a shark but perfect for the scum below.

With the tightening of her chest muscles, Riddle triggered her weapon to discharge. She watched with intense satisfaction as the small harpoon whistled through the night.

"Ah HAH!" She smiled as she heard the impact of her first shot followed by the splashing of a man fed to the sharks he worshipped moments before.

They did not stand a chance under her watch, and she continued to fire until all of them disappeared in the churning waters below, harpoons driven deep.

"*Riddle!*" Mr. Pit screamed.

Riddle peered below. Her eyes squinted into slits as she tried to see if any more attempted to climb up. "Clear!" She reported back.

"Switch places with Coral, she's struggling to keep up with them."

"Aye-aye!"

Riddle's boots pounded against the deck as she sped to relieve Coral. Sure enough, the side of the ship she was on crawled with the cultists. Mr. Pit lit an oil lamp and used mirrors to direct the beam on the side of the ship, sweeping across to highlight any intruders.

Coral hesitated when Riddle took over. She stood there for a moment and watched Riddle in amazement. Click. Click. Click. Riddle's weapon snapped in a steady rhythm. Some of the men were able to avoid her deadly aim, but it wasn't enough to save them from her next shot. Coral broke herself away and ran with her bow to the opposite side of the ship.

Drucilla steered the *Penny Dreadful* as far away from Croatoa's entrance point as possible. They were still too far away from the main hoard to use any of their big weapons. In the distance, Captain Dru could see the people of Seattle defending their docks by whatever means they could.

The most difficult part about the swarm was that they spread out like fingers through the waves. There was no central mass to direct attention to. The cultists moved as they pleased without rhyme or reason. They were chaotically scattered about and focusing their efforts on whatever was most destructive and close by. They boarded the other whaling vessels and swarmed the docks. Drucilla pulled the *Penny Dreadful* alongside a small crabbing ship that had appeared out of the half-sunken press of skyscrapers on the edge of the battlefield.

Vladimir noticed it first. The Panzer's had overwhelmed the crabbing vessel as they drew near, the valiant even if ill-advised attack having only served to whip the cult warriors into a frenzy. The screams of a woman cut through the air as they approached. There were at least fifteen cultists on the top decks of the fishing vessel, only a handful of them having fallen in the bloody melee to seize the deck. Most of the reinforcements attacking the *Penny* diverted their energy to the crab vessel. The cultists were as bad about losing themselves in a feeding frenzy as the sharks were, thought Mr. Pit as he watched with a twist in his guts as shark and cultist alike converged on the dying ship. This did however give a momentary reprieve for the *Penny*.

Mr. Pit signaled for another team of archers. Just as they did at the village, the archers laid out on their backs and used their specialized bows. They hooked them around their feet and used their cores to release wave after wave of arrows to rain down upon the crab boat. They did not cease fire until Mr. Pit signaled for them to stop.

"Riddle!"

"Yes, sir!"

"Commandeer that ship!" Mr. Pit commanded.

Riddle was short and slender but as tough they came. Normally she stayed on the ship to keep the men in line. Yes, she was able to hunt with the others, but it was her duty to protect the *Penny Dreadful* and keep the crew in line. A line was shot across the crab vessel for her. She used her mechanical arm to slide across the ropes connecting the two ships.

The small crab boat was scattered with blood and corpses. Riddle stepped on both fisherman and Panzer Fish without discrimination as she made her way to the wheel house. She couldn't stop smiling as she pulled the ship closer to the *Penny Dreadful*. More lines shot across, and it wasn't long before a small team accompanied Riddle on the crabbing boat along with two of Vladimir's catapults. Riddle let out a wild laugh.

"Hit them with whatever you find! Start with their buddies corpses!" She screamed.

Unlike the *Penny Dreadful*, she steered in an open space that allowed the salt and wind to sweep her hair about her like fire. The small group of men under her command obeyed. They targeted anyone getting close to the *Penny Dreadful*, hurtling corpses at the Panzer Fish trying to board. It wasn't long until the waters immediately around them were cleared enough to focus on actually helping Seattle.

17.

As Croatoa led his group of divers through the underwater streets, approaching where he thought the concentration of Panzer Fish would be an explosion somewhere ahead under the water sent a tsunami through the group.

The force of the blast caused an intense undercurrent, throwing the men in different directions and stunning them. The concussion caused buildings around them to collapse and debris started falling through the water and crashing into them. Croatoa was thrown into a brick wall.

The water was impossible to see through following the explosion. Croatoa tried to catch his breath and breathe through the pain spreading from his back through his whole body. He kept shifting his gaze around him, hoping the visibility would clear for him to see. His skin crawled knowing that danger could be lurking a foot in front of his face, and there was no way he would be able to tell until the sand settled back down again.

When the murky ocean started to clear, Croatoa became aware of something he should have accounted for. He planned for the cultists and the sharks, but he forgot that the crabs would be drawn in from their normal feeding grounds by the blood and carnage. The filthy scavengers were larger than some of the cars. As they closed in, Sailor Dave tried to block each swing of a claw. He was used to hunting from above, not below.

As a crab cornered Croatoa he thrust with his lance, attempting to stave of the pinching claws of the crustacean.

Bard ran up the back of the shell as fast as he and thrust his marlin spike hard into the back of the giant crab's neck. The huge shelled creature stumbled and collapsed, sending up another cloud of dust. Sailor Dave barely escaped its fall.

Croatoa looked around. Chimp hovered in the broken remains of a bank's double doors. At first it appeared there was another one of our men directly behind him, but the shadow grew larger than Chimp. Croatoa pointed, frantically gesturing in an attempt to warn the man. Chimp turned his head over his shoulder just in time to see the jaws of a great white shark split him in two.

The shark shook Chimp's body back and forth, bashing him against the faux concrete pillars outlining the entrance. Sailor Dave was the first to move. Chimp and he were not particularly close friends, but they had worked side by side for years together on the *Penny Dreadful*. He pushed off the cracked and algae-slicked asphalt and glided through the water with lance ready. The hyper intelligent shark backed away into the darkness of the building just as Sailor's lance came down.

He missed. His lance lodged itself in a crack in the cement. Croatoa and Bard watched, expecting the shark to attack him in the brief seconds he stumbled. The shark's gigantic, black eyes met Sailor's. As if the beast knew what it was doing to Sailor mentally, it kept Chimp's mangled body in between its teeth and backed up, luring Dave into the dark confines of the bank. Croatoa tried to motion for him to return to the group, to get the fuck out, to avoid the dark dilapidated interior of the bank, but the sight of Chimp's body dangling limp from the great white's mouth was too much for him to bear.

The visibility was getting better, but the crabs were swarming into the center of the city to feed off the body parts and carcasses drifting down from the battle above. Croatoa and Bard were left with no other choice and went into the bank after Sailor Dave, armed and ready for an attack. To surprise, as soon as they made it past the threshold of the bank, it appeared as if the shark disappeared completely.

Croatoa motioned for them to keep their backs towards one another for a full 360 view of their surroundings. He tried to encourage Sailor to abandon Chimp and draw the shark out into the open where there was more light. They did not have the spare air for this delay. Without being able to call out direct commands, Croatoa was helpless against the vengeful determination of his crew member. The shark drew them deeper into the open rooms of the bank.

The first room was large with high ceilings. Long rectangle strips cut through the room. The glass was long gone from the windows, but they still allowed a bit of light to penetrate the bank's interior. There was no shark in sight. All three of them looked about for a sign of the beast. Bard spotted him and grabbed Sailor Dave's shoulder and pointed to where there appeared to be the flickering of a fin or a tail or something in the darkness of a hallway.

Croatoa knew how dangerous this was. He knew he was responsible. He thought of the explosion that just sounded, and how another was sure to follow. Despite knowing how dangerous what they were doing was, there was no way he could abandon Sailor, especially considering the rest of his team, other than Tak, who at last emerged from the debris cloud unscathed, had been lost to the explosion. A horrible start. He tried reminding himself that this was part of the job, if they didn't kill this bastard shark, it would kill someone else. He just hated being lured like this into the buildings.

The hall was wide and stretched out until it disappeared into complete darkness. There were doors lining the hall. Some of them were closed, some of them were obstructed by debris from when the bank went out of business during the Great Melt. Bard brought out his light stick. It was an ingenious invention. Vladimir had brought it to the *Penny Dreadful*, but skilled as he was, he did not have the knowledge to make them, and had traded untold fortunes to secure them from traders that came up from the South China sea every few years. They used bacteria and phosphorescent plankton. The *Penny Dreadful* was one of the few ships to own more than one of them.

His light penetrated the darkness all around them as he waved the stick into one of the neighboring rooms. The face of the massive shark was mere feet in front of him, bits of Chimp still dangling from its mouth. Bard fell back into the hall with Croatoa and Sailor. It was as if the shark had been there, waiting in the darkness to be noticed, like some sick game of hide and seek. The light stick fell to the floor along with Bard.

Sailor Dave lunged at the shark with his lance. The shark opened its great mouth and attempted to smash down on the long spear. Dave withdrew it just in time to avoid losing his weapon and parried again. Croatoa moved in front of Bard, armed with a Marlin spike and a crow bar.

Bard's fingers fumbled in the loose sand for the light stick. The sand shifted over the light, temporarily casting the group into darkness. Once his thick gloves curled around the bright tube, it took mere seconds to attach it onto his belt and join the fight.

Vladimir had outfitted Bard with a special device similar to Riddle's mini-harpoon attachment. This was larger though and much more deadly, albeit time consuming to load. Bard loaded a long harpoon into the machine blindly, cranking the mechanism to pull the harpoon back, eyes trained on the beast and his three companions.

Croatoa and Sailor Dave fought ferociously in an attempt to keep the shark occupied long enough for Bard to take action. He lined up the harpoon with the gigantic black eyes of the shark, took one calming breath and fired.

The shark's face exploded into a cloud of blood. The harpoon penetrated its eye, but it wasn't enough. The creature flailed, knocking Sailor Dave and Tak over with the mass of its body. The shark powered past them, plowing them down in an attempt to escape. All four of the men were had brought whaling hooks, and Sailor Dave swung his with all his might as Tak struggled to untangle himself from wires protruding from the shattered wall.

Dave's hook sunk into the armored flesh of the great white. He knocked Croatoa over as the shark pulled him through the hallway by the short rope affixed to the bottom of the hook. Croatoa and Brad reacted swiftly, and thanks to the delay of the first hook, they managed to sink their's into the beast's tail. The shark's speed slowed down with the added weight of all three of the men. It started to zigzag down the passageway, swinging them into each other and into the walls. They held on, trying to keep from breaking a limb in the process. Their diving bells protected their skulls as they were thrown like ragdolls against the solid walls.

A gigantic crab awaited the shark in the main entrance, feeding on Chimp's corpse. The giant crab raised its humongous claws up and thrust it into the face of the great white shark. The mutated crustacean blocked the only way for the shark to escape.

Croatoa stabbed the shark's back with his spike, twisting it in between two armored plates. The shark reacted by violently tossing its body side by side. The predator couldn't attack Croatoa and Dave without falling victim to the enormous crab fighting against it with all of its might. Croatoa cut Bard's line giving him a chance to load another harpoon. Dave and Croatoa stabbed at the shark repeatedly. The crab attacked the shark's side and nearly pincered Dave along with the flesh of the great white. If it wasn't for Croatoa pulling him out of the claw's grasps, he would have lost his entire leg.

Precious seconds raced by as Bard waited for the perfect moment. A miss could easily kill Croatoa, Dave or even the crab and they needed that crab alive until the shark was completely defeated. Croatoa looked back and saw Bard was ready. He motioned for Dave to be prepared to dismount from the shark. They withdrew their hooks from the beast, still keeping their weapons hooked into its side. Bard fired again and the second harpoon shot into the belly of the beast.

Guts spilled over the floor followed by the massive carcass. Dave and Croatoa leaped from the creature just in time to avoid becoming a part of the crab's meal. With the giant shark dead, the crab seemed to be oblivious to the four of them as Tak finally re-joined the group. Croatoa motioned for them to move around the crustacean and leave him there to feed off the shark's corpse. They were already exhausted, and there was still more to be done before their air supply ran empty.

18.

Up above, on the ocean's surface, the *Penny Dreadful* picked off the Panzer Fish methodically, their vast experience as whalers giving them the discipline to grind through the battle with precision and patience under fire. Each unit had a specific job and knew what they were to do. More archers flooded over to Riddle's commandeered ship. The men and women who boarded with her before separating from the *Penny Dreadful* knew what risks they were taking being under her command. She was a killer, not a captain, and that's what the *Penny* needed in order to draw enemy attention away from the larger ship and the Seattle docks.

Drucilla kept an eye on Riddle's boat, cautious not to get too close to her, as the plan was working perfectly, and the enemy were swarming the smaller vessel. Riddle's small crew fought like furies as they drove the Panzers back into in the water. Whenever a group of the cultists collected too close together on their assault vessels, the small band would load the catapult with some of the corpses on the crabbing boat, light them on fire with whale oil, and hurl them at the Panzers. Even if they were only knocked from their jet skis, the oil fueled fire was bright enough to illuminate their positions in the water for the archers to finish off. Sadly this also meant that in addition to keeping the cultists from overrunning the crab boat, Riddle's hastily assembled crew had to contend with the accidental fires spreading across the deck from their own catapult.

On the *Penny Dreadful*, Artisema worked with Vladimir. He had created twenty-six water proof ordinance pods for the battle, and the young girl knew that the entire salvage hold of the ship was now picked clean. It was Artisema's idea to bait them and make them float. The small explosives were lodged in the center of buoys. Each buoy was contained inside of a mesh bait bag. Artisema shoved her tiny hands into a pail filled with small fish. She threw them on the deck and bashed them with a hammer. The fresh fish was tossed into the bait bags and sealed off.

Vladimir took the buoy and submerged it into a vat of potent smelling blood. The thick, red liquid oozed all over the device. Vladimir loaded it up into the catapult. Artisema would aim towards a group of sharks conglomerating together, far enough away from the other vessels to avoid damage.

"You think it will work?" she asked.

Vladimir shrugged his shoulders and pulled the lever back, releasing the catapult. The make-shift bomb hurtled through the air and landed in the middle of a swarm. Within seconds of landing a massive shark ripped at the buoy setting off the explosion. Bits of shark exploded into the air. Artisema and Vladimir laughed in jubilant delight, though as the sheer size of the shark's mangled body became apparent, they both went quiet. It was huge, beyond anything they'd seen so far. Not nearly the size of the Mega, but more than they'd seen thus far. The Panzers had truly harnessed some epic monsters for this mighty siege.

Mr. Pit continued to watch the docks and structures of Seattle. It was hard to tell, under the cloak of darkness and in spite of the enemy's fishbone armor, who was a Panzer and who was a Seattle citizen. It seemed as if many of the people were hidden within the city's structures. He could spot a few burly men trying to keep the Panzer Fish from bashing down a metal door here, or meeting them blade on blade amongst the rigging that lined some of the other buildings, but there were so many entrance points and not enough people to guard them. Where the cultists did penetrate the city, Mr. Pit could see them raiding the buildings for supplies and emptying the homes of their occupants.

Drucilla saw this as well. "Get, Mr. Pit for me," Drucilla whispered to a thin, tall man standing beside her. He was there for the exact purpose of running messages. His name was Rover, aptly named as he was the fastest man on the ship. It was not long before he returned with Mr. Pit.

"Captain."

"What can we do about that? I fear that our long range weapons will kill just as many of our people as theirs."

Mr. Pit pursed his lips. His weight shifted from the balls of his feet to his heels and then back again. "We don't have the man power to send skirmishers, Drucilla." Dru could see the disappointment in his face as he told her the truth, "I'm sorry. You want my honest advice, we focus on clearin' the waters. Get those rootin' bastards to turn tail or drown. You can't be responsible for all of Seattle. They need to fight too."

Drucilla bit her lip. She knew it was true. Drucilla turned the helm to avoid a swarm of sharks. "What the fuck are Vlad and that girl doing?"

Mr. Pit smiled. The view from the wheel house obstructed her from seeing the shark explosions before that point. She saw the buoy, and then watched it explode. The wheel house was close enough to have a light misting of blood rain in with the salty breeze.

"Oh my," she said, visibly impressed, "Alright, I'm going to pull the ship closer into the bay. Have half the archers focus on keeping the pressure off our exposed flank. Have the rest prepared to broadside any of those cult bastards they can off Seattle's shores. Let Vlad and the girl continue as they are. The sharks can't swim onto those docks, and as long as Croatoa makes good, they'll never get the chance. "

"Aye-aye, Captain."

The smell of sulfur filled the air. Drucilla was right to be concerned about her people. Few of them were able to sleep before the battle. Even manning the catapults was physically exhausting. Hours passed, and still, the waters bucked with more Panzer Fish than they had ever seen at one time.

Drucilla focused on steering the ship. She tried to hug it close to the shore. The cultists would deploy various tactics to push her away and provide an opening for the invasion. It took Drucilla's complete concentration to keep the ship out of danger while still conducting an attack. Drucilla yawned. Her eyes burned, and even though she had the luxury to sit, she was still exhausted.

Artisema looked to Vlad, "This is the last one."

Vladimir looked out at the waters.

Dorsal fins still scattered in the bright roving lights of the *Penny Dreadful.*

"I wish we could have made more."

19.

When Croatoa imagined protecting the structures, he didn't realize what it would be like in truth. He thought if he stood in the middle of Seattle, around Pike's Place, he would see the divers and take them out before they could lay any more of the devastating explosives. The problem lay in the fact that Seattle was huge, and the Panzer Fish attacked without any semblance of overall strategy, making them impossible to predict. They spent the majority of their time following the sounds of random buildings being taken out.

It took what felt like an hour to see another shark. As they drew near, more and more of the scene became visible. There were three sharks in total surrounding a group of three divers. They took cover behind a truck lying on its side. In the distance the grainy silhouettes of another small group of divers could be made out at the next building down.

Croatoa looked up. It was worse than he had imagined. The two buildings they chose were at central points of new Seattle's structure. If they were to blow up one, half of Pike's Place would collapse along with the connecting docks. A large amount of structures would be unfixed, including private homes, and would probably wash right out to sea. The second one was similar to the first, a crux point. It wouldn't be just one structure—it would damage huge portions of the city.

They were outnumbered, with no signs of the rest of their dive team, lost in the explosion.

The first order would be to distract and kill the sharks. It appeared as if the Panzer Fish were not prepared with weapons at all, choosing instead to load up with the tools of their mission. Their arms carried lights and explosives and they had their diving gear, and that was it beyond the basic knives on their belts.

Bard gave Croatoa the miniature harpoon gun. It was clear to everyone, who would slip in and dispose of the explosives. Bard ran his hands over his suit, ensuring his knives were still in each holster. Vladimir gave him a single explosive for emergencies, a gas bomb that would likely only affect the sharks, as it would fill their gills with pressurized gas and suffocate them.

Bard caught Croatoa's arm, keeping him from firing away at the sharks and showed him the gas bomb. Croatoa nodded. Bard did his best to explain a plan in crude sign language. He pointed to Sailor and gestured for him to circle around the buildings and sneak up on the far set of cultists and for Croatoa to stay put and use the harpoon gun.

Everyone seemed to be on the same page. Sailor split off, mirroring Bard, as they approached the group of men trying to decide where to attach their explosives. The darkness beyond the perimeter of light being used by the Panzers provided concealment as Bard approached. The Panzer's weren't the problem though, it was the sharks. They hovered above their wards, casting ominous black silhouettes on the illuminated, ancient city walls.

Bard kept his eyes trained on the men. The closer he came, the less shadows there were but the bomb wouldn't travel far in the water and had to be close. When he didn't dare go any further, scared the gray light would alert the sharks of his presence, he paused, heart pounding. Once they took notice, it would be over. There would be a small delay before the gas bomb went off and Bard needed the element of surprise for this to work.

Taking a deep breath to steady himself steady, he saw Croatoa tighten his grip on the cranked up harpoon gun. Bard took a deep breath and pulled the trigger pin on the grenade and lobbed it as hard as he could.

The sharks reacted to the movement the instant the device left his hand. He yanked the harpoon out as they turned on him. The next seconds slowed down. It felt as if they were taking forever to get close enough for Bard to hit them. Their eyes were black and shiny as polished buttons and they radiated hunger.

One of Croatoa's harpoons hit the smallest of the three in the face. The shark stopped moving and actually started to sink to the bottom. A large part of him feared the gas wouldn't even work, and then it exploded near the two oncoming monsters. As the question entered Bard's mind the other two sharks went slack in the water and sanks to the street below, visibly asphyxiating. Even though Sailor Dave was well concealed, the divers now knew that somewhere in the impenetrable black, more threats awaited. Croatoa and Bard were still somewhat hidden by the dark waters, but the cultists knew what directions the attack came from.

Bard hovered close to the walls where it was darkest, readjusted the grip on his spear and hoped they would investigate. One of the men took a couple steps outside of the ring of light. It was seconds before he returned, blinded by the sudden change. Bard could see them communicate to one another. To his dismay they set four people to guard all directions instead of exploring the darkness, revealing that the *Penny* divers had missed several of the divers in the gloom, the war party being larger than anticipated. The rest of them returned to staking out the places to put the explosives.

It would not be long now before they decided on which support beams would take down the buildings. The buildings themselves were not impressive. That is why they were used as a foundation for the junction in the docks connecting the structures, and the lightest portion of Pike's Place. One of Croatoa's harpoons spit out and nailed the guard closest to them in the head. His diving helmet cracked and blood started spreading in the water.

Croatoa only had a few miniature harpoons left. He did have another weapon, a good weapon, on him. It was for emergencies though. The modified nail gun ran off of compressed air. His back pack was equipped to run it, but it meant siphoning his personal air into the gun. Croatoa counted the bolts he had left. Three shots remained.

When the man on watch fell, the other men on guard zoomed in on their position. Bard, Tak, and Sailor Dave were ready for them. The guard from the east came first. Croatoa picked off the next closest, giving the others a moment to close distance.

Bard's spear dragged through the water. The Panzer was wielding a long, thin blade that cut through the water like butter. The metal plates wrapped around Bard's spear were of more use than the actual spear head. With the drag of the water, it was difficult and exhausting to meet each blow and nearly impossible to control an attack until the cultist tired. Bard knew he needed to drop the spear and switch to his knives, but in the flurry of the hostile's attack there was no time.

Croatoa discharged another harpoon. It sliced through the water just in front of the Panzer Fish's face. Although Croatoa missed it was enough to stall the man. Bard seized the opportunity and thrust his spear into the belly of the diver. Croatoa's last harpoon hit the next attacker in the shoulder. Bard secured the spear. Fast as lightening, he whipped out his two sleekest blades. The body of another diver drifted nearby, impaled by Sailor Dave's spear even as the large man and another cult diver slashed at each other with short knives.

Tak managed to bury his spear into the cultist as he flanked the hostile diver, though no sooner had Tak gutted the man Sailor Dave had been fighting, another diver streaked past him. As the cult diver moved along, he dragged a dark colored club across Tak's back. It appeared to be coated with some kind of poisonous fish spine, as the Penny diver immediately began to convulse and spew red-tinged bubbles as he began seizing so hard the sounds of his bones breaking could be heard under the deep.

The Panzer Fish rushed Bard as Sailor Dave tried in vain to help the dying Tak, but then stalled under the impact of Croatoa's harpoon, touching the spot where it thrust clean through him. Blood clouded out like small puffs of vapor. Bard jumped in, knives slashed in a vengeful fury before Panzer Fish had time to strike with his deadly weapon. The Panzer Fish fell back. His bat-wielding arm lifted into the air as he fell.

The needles dusted the inside of Bard's forearm with the lightest touch and he was relieved to see the suit did not tear under the poisonous spines. As he looked for damage, the place where the spines had brushed the neoprene suddenly began to bubble alarmingly.

There was nothing Bard could do except wait to see if the poison would reach his skin. To his great relief the catalyst stopped reacting with the rubber, leaving a thin but unbroken spot. It would tear if he moved wrong but the suit remained sealed.

Croatoa appeared from the darkness wielding the nail gun which was now sharing his air. They had been beneath the waves much longer than they initially expected. Although they were here on the cusp of returning to the surface's battle, there was no telling how much longer they would need air for. Bard pointed at Croatoa and made a shrugging motion. Croatoa swiped at the water in front of him, motioning for him to forget about it. He made a "go on" gesture, commanding Bard and Sailor Dave to move forward. They'd been too late to save the first building, and lost more than half the dive team in the explosion, this time there were bombs to dismantle.

20.

The *Penny Dreadful* still sailed unscathed. Men kept the engines fueled and running, eating through the stores of oil from their last catch. The smell of whale oil mingled with the sulfur from weapons, and the burning of the buildings. The men and women aboard the ship were exhausted. They had collectively killed hundreds of sharks and dozens of cultists. It seemed as if they kept appearing from the ocean waves. The thought of revenge drove her to keep fighting and encouraging her crew to push on.

In the distance, the Panzer Fish managed to set two boats on fire from the docks. One of them was the small crab vessel Riddle commandeered. Riddle had pulled the ship in close to the docks, allowing her small command to do serious damage to the Panzer Fish terrorizing the floating structure as well as the ones attempting to invade from the sea, not to mention drawing off enough of the enemy to buy time for the lone surviving whaleship to break free from the bay and into open ocean. Most of the men and women that had boarded along with Riddle were dead from the fighting, though the handful of survivors abandoned ship as soon as the boat caught fire. Riddle screamed into the howling wind, over the sounds of the boat's engines exploding before jumping into the cold, black, water.

Right into the shark swarm.

It had been a suicide run and all of them knew it before boarding, but that didn't make Riddle any less furious to lose.

The fire cast enough light for Riddle to see the dangers surrounding her. Dorsal fins of sharks broke the surface, coming toward her. Even though she was strong for being so petite, her mechanical arm was heavy and it was difficult for Riddle to swim. There was enough debris floating by to help keep her afloat. She threw her heavy arm onto a plank of sturdy wood and used it to stabilize herself as she fired at the sharks growing near.

From the deck of the *Penny Dreadful*, Artisema spotted Riddle in the water. She ran as fast as she could to adjust the mirrors and put the spotlight directly on her.

"ARCHERS! ON RIDDLE! PORT SIDE!" She screamed over the raging battle, her voice powerful enough that the archers who yet had arrows to fire did not hesitate in following her orders in the heat of the moment.

Artisema knitted her brow and kept her eyes trained on Riddle's small figure standing on a half-submerged plank of wood, firing for all she was worth. Artisema kept the light on her at all times, illuminating the shark's dorsal fins and showing the archers where to aim. Bolts rained down on the sharks surrounding Riddle.

Riddle could hear the roar of a jet ski behind her. She turned in the water, relying on the trust she had for her shipmates aboard the *Penny Dreadful*. She aimed her mechanical arm at the dreaded Panzer Fish driving it and despite the swell of the water she still cut right through his eye, though not before his hand crossbow fired back. The jet ski spun out of control as the rider fell into the sea. Riddle doubled her efforts. The sharks were close behind, an ominous presence in the water.

Just as Riddle's hand grabbed onto the jet ski, she realized that her leg wasn't working, and looked down to see that the cultist's bolt had sunk deep into her thigh. She screamed out but she was still able to move, although the arrow in her leg rendered it useless for helping her onto the jet ski. She managed to pull it towards her in the water and flip it right side up. She struggled, knowing there wasn't much time left. It took all of her strength to drag herself onto the jet ski, blood spilling down her leg. She looked over her shoulder at the fins swimming towards her then tried to gun the engine only to have it sputter. Cursing, she tried again and the jet ski lurched forward as two of angry sharks burst form the water.

She wasn't out of danger yet. The sharks were still racing after her. Artisema kept the spot light trained on her. While it allowed the *Penny Dreadful*'s crew to try and keep her safe from the sharks so they could fire upon them, it also made Riddle a target for the handful of Panzers that still stalked the chaotic battlefield. Bullets, arrows, and hooks split into the ocean all around Riddle, some pinging off the jet ski as she shot through the waves. The *Penny Dreadful* was close. She just needed to survive a little longer. Riddle weaved back and forth, unevenly zig-zagging to prevent making herself an easy target. The cult was swarming towards her, eager to take revenge against the temporary crab boat captain who had all but broken their assault's momentum.

She was able to avoid the attacks from the docks. However, she could hear jet skis coming up behind her. She dared a look over her shoulder and saw two. One took a shot in the shoulder and tumbled from his jet ski.

The second Panzer Fish was closing in fast. Riddle looked ahead at the ship, dead ahead, a ladder swinging from the side. There was no time to slow down. She grit her teeth, steered the jet ski into a sideways slide that almost slammed it into the ship and jumped for the ladder. To fall would mean death. Her hand hit the rope of the ladder and she grabbed frantically at it with her one hand but it slipped through her fingers. She thought it was over when a shriek came from above her and she saw Artisema hurtling towards her, a coil of rope unrolling behind her.

Artisema caught Riddle in a desperate grab around her waist just as the rope played out leaving them both barely dangling in the water with the ladder next to them swinging back and forth with every violent rock of the ship. The Panzer on the jet ski grabbed Riddle by her bad leg and did his best to pull her free. Artisema clung to Riddle's waist in a death grip, shouting gibberish. Riddle screamed as the marauder grabbed onto the arrow in her calf and ripped it out, blood sprayed into the water, drawing the sharks closer. Desperate hands hauled Artisema's rope from above, while the archer's, still firing, tried not to injure Riddle or Artisema.

Riddle managed to kick out with her uninjured leg and knock the Panzer's hand from her other ankle. Artisema found the strength from somewhere to twist them both so that Riddle was against the ladder and she grabbed hold of it twisting her arm through the ropes. Artisema let her go and was instantly hauled back up. As the Panzer leaped from his jet ski in a last attempt to bring her down she twisted and pulled the trigger on her mechanical arm. The sharpened blade on the end punched into his head as his hand slid up her thigh. Blood spluttered from his gargling mouth. He looked at Riddle with wide disbelief before he fell back into the water and as food for the sharks.

21.

The divers within the building were done with planting the bombs on the structures, so focused on their task that they'd not noticed the death of the rest of their war party or pet sharks. Croatoa and Bard the cultists with lightning speed. As the others fought, Sailor Dave was able to sneak around them from his hiding place in the darkness.

The two structures were across a small, narrow road from one another. As Croatoa and Bard engaged the divers, Sailor Dave climbed in through an apartment window. It did not take him long to find where the charges were. The device was smeared with a phosphorescent blue algae that produced enough light for the cultists to work on the explosives in utter darkness.

The simple whaler looked at the strange mechanism. He could see the hands cycling swiftly on the small face of the windup clock but there was no telling how much time was left. Sailor Dave was not much for counting, but he had at least secured the location of the bombs. He had no idea how to disarm it but if they was probably gonna all die anyway and it didn't look like Bard was gonna get there in time, anything was better than nothing.

He scrunched his eyes shut and ripped all of the wires out.

Nothing happened and when he cracked open one eye the clock had stopped ticking.

Taking a few seconds to he quit shaking, Sailor Dave finally rushed as fast as he could out of the dingy, brick apartments. He stood the threshold of the door leading back into the street. Before he around the corner, he listened intently. He could hear the dulled sound of clashing steel closer to him than before. When he peeked around the corner he could see five men battling in the distance. It was difficult for Sailor Dave to tell who was who with the low visibility and everyone wearing diving gear. With their superior numbers it appeared that the Panzers had driven Bard and Croatoa across the street, until Sailor Dave remembered that Croatoa had pointed at both buildings. That's right Dave, two sets of bombs.

It took the whaler a moment to time his swim across the road. It was better if the cultists were completely ignorant of his existence, especially with them fighting so close to him now. There was less time than the other one. Sailor hurried through room after room looking for the telltale phosphorescent glow. This one wasn't as easy as in the apartments. There were odd corridors and hallways twisting here and there, creating a confusing labyrinth.

There was no way to tell what kind of structure this was intended for. Dave knew up ahead it supported the main junction adjoining Seattle's most traveled docks. In the very center of the building there was a great column erected in the middle of a large, square room. Attached to the column, Dave found the bombs ticking away. The hands on the clock were cycling madly.

Sailor Dave took a deep breath. He was here. He made it. All he needed to do was remove the wires like he did with the last one. The knife he carried with him had a broad, wide blade. Dave cut the wires from the ordinance and removed it from the column.

To his dismay, the clock did not stop. Maybe he should have ripped them out like last time. He tried, but now the wires were too short to get a good grip with his huge hands.

There was a brief moment of shock when he looked at the explosive in his arms, dumbfounded. Dave's feet moved almost before his mind consciously decided on what he had to do.

As he moved through the water in what seemed like an agony of slowness, the device gripped in both hands.

Sailor Dave moved as fast as he could, his powerful legs kicking stroked that propelled him faster through the water than most men could manage. Past where Croatoa and Bard still battled with the Panzer Fish. He took a left. He took a right, into one of the collapsed building, as far as he could get inside until his way was blocked by a stone wall.

Then he did the only thing he could think of. He crushed himself into the corner as tightly as he could and wrapping his body around the explosive.

As the clock ticked down he pictured himself standing on the Penny Dreadful as a cool salty breeze swept across the boat.

He locked the image in his head and closed his eyes.

22.

When the explosion came, it was a muffled boom under the water, it caused a strong undercurrent that rippled throughout the city's grim structures but there was only slight damage created to the walls surrounding the courtyard above on the ocean's surface.

The rush of energy below hit the fighters with a violent impact. The cultist Croatoa fought against slammed into the brick wall parallel to him. His head flattened from the force of the blast pounding his brains into the apartment building. Croatoa was carried far down the street with the strong wave.

It seemed as if Croatoa would end up on the other side of Seattle with the force by which he'd been thrown. He was headed for a set of doors, and grabbed onto the threshold as he passed and tried to hold on with all his might, waiting for the wave to move past him. He had not seen where Bard had been thrown and the water around him was solid grey with sand and debris from the blast.

When the aftermath of the explosion calmed, the ocean was once again cast in a grainy darkness as the accumulated silt, rust, and algae clouded the already dark waters. It was difficult for Croatoa to even see his hand as he waved it in front of his face. He found his light stick, not needing to worry about the underwater Panzer Fish terrorists seeing him now. He used the bright light to illuminate his air gage. The gage told him what he already knew—he would run out of air soon.

The crabber detached the nail gun from his air supply. There was no way he could use it, even in an emergency. It would eat the little bit of oxygen he had left. He needed to get to the surface as fast as his body would allow him. Croatoa grew up crabbing in Seattle. There was one thing he learned early on about diving. It was a necessity to remain calm. Instead of hurrying as fast as he could to the surface, he took the moment for the visibility to clear to check over what weapons remained in his possession.

There were two blades in his utility belt. Croatoa started the mission with five. He started with a marlin spike and a crowbar.

He started with an air-powered nail gun. Now he had two knives and less than an hour's worth of oxygen to help him get back to the surface. It would not take him that long to get up to the surface. There was no way he could abandon Bard or Sailor Dave without looking for them. Bard and Croatoa had always been close. Bard slept beneath Croatoa in the bunk house and would spin tale after tale after tale for his enjoyment. He saved Croatoa's life in many situations. Sailor Dave was loved by all, a steady whaler and friend.

It was an easy decision. Croatoa would search for ten of the twenty minutes he had left and then begin his ascension to the surface. The middle aged man moved as fast as he could to the spot where they were separated. When he approached the place where they spent so much time battling the cultist divers, he could see the mashed in face of the Panzer Fish he had fought. It was like raw hamburger, inverted into itself with skull fragments like maggots spotting the red bubbling flesh. Small scavengers were already at work on him.

Croatoa gagged at the sight of the cultist's face and prayed to himself he wouldn't find Bard in a similar state. He was just about to walk into the building when the hairs on the back of his neck pricked and sent a tingling sensation surging down his spine. Croatoa turned around slowly. Big, black, soulless eyes met his. It was the same shark as before. He could see one of his harpoons lodged into one of the armor plates. It had survived the gas, and the monster had come to exact its revenge.

Croatoa's heart dropped.

He jerked back barely missed being snatched by the jaws of the angry beast snapping down on him. If it was not for the narrow entrance into the apartment complex, he would have found himself chewed alive by the angry shark. The creature was gigantic—a tank with long pink scars all over its body from fights he had survived. Croatoa ran down the hallway, hoping to find an exit on the other side. He could hear the creature behind him.

The apartment's narrow threshold was merely a deterrent for the beast. The hyper intelligent creature was not just ravenous for human flesh, it was actively stalking him. Croatoa only looked into the shark's eyes for a brief second, but he could see the recognition. The bastard knew Croatoa was the cause of the harpoon in its side. He knew that Croatoa was to blame for the gas. The shark backed up and rammed itself into the entrance. The brick walls shook.

At the end of the hallway, Croatoa was met with a dead end. There was no way out other than through the door now being rammed to pieces by the monster. The shark slammed itself into the door way again. This time the bricks crumbled away from the weak wooden frame. The crabber looked around him, sure that the building would collapse with the loss of the wall.

With nowhere left to go, Croatoa bounded up a set of stairs to his left. The shark still could not get in, even with the door being widened by a few feet. He was a huge creature. Croatoa's mind raced with all the ways he may be able to escape. The shark was fast and smart. He was somewhat safe for the time being within the walls of the apartment complex.

The bricks could be damaged and knocked away, but the shark would hardly fit into any of the rooms, even if he was able to force himself through. Croatoa checked his air gauge. He was cutting time close. If he could just slow the shark down or find something to kill it with, he could escape to the surface, and then perhaps free dive over and over into the area until he found his companions. Assuming he could find a way to defeat the shark.

Croatoa ran from apartment to apartment looking for anything that may help him defeat the shark. Every apartment he went into, the shark could be seen lurking outside of the windows, trying to force his way inside with brute strength. Most of the apartment buildings contained nothing of use, and he counted himself lucky not to have stumbled upon more crabs. Divers had been coming down for over eighty years, stripping the buildings clean of everything. Weapons were almost impossible to find in obvious places like old apartment complexes or houses.

Croatoa swam up and up and up through the ruined building. His feet led him into one especially large apartment on a floor near the top of the building. It did not look like the kind of place he would be able to find salvation. It was clean and sterile compared to the other apartments. Most of the living spaces were filled with wet, animal eaten curtains, remnants of couches now housing various aquatic plants, and the carcasses of luxury items now used for breeding grounds for weird fish.

The apartment he stood in now was not like that. There was nothing in it except the basics. There was no furniture. There were no decorations or elements suggesting anyone lived there at all. Something about the place drew Croatoa in deeper. With the other apartments he would give a quick run through looking for spots that looked as if they had not been disturbed by humans yet. If he found the doors ajar and the pantries empty and everything open, he would move onto the next apartment. This apartment was clearly like this long before the Melt.

All of the doors were closed still. It looked as if people gave it a quick look over and abandoned it as a lost cause because of how bare it appeared. Croatoa went into the first rooms. One had a heavy steel work table bolted into the floor. It was in this room that he noticed something odd. There were no closets like the other rooms. Unlike the other rooms, this room had furniture. Croatoa pulled on the table. It did not budge. He knocked on the wall behind it. A hollow, muted echo moved through the water. There was a room or a closet or something behind the table.

Another muffled crash sounded just outside the window. Croatoa looked over to see the drab gray body of the shark slamming into the side of the building. Croatoa looked at the bolts. There was nothing particularly special about them. They were rusted and brittle. He looked around once more, as if magically all the tools needed would appear before him. They did not, of course. The shark hit the wall protecting Croatoa once more, causing the room to vibrate beneath the blow.

Croatoa looked at his air tank. It was low. It was too low. Croatoa normally wouldn't risk injuring any kind of weapon or tool, especially one as useful as the nail gun he wielded. This was not any occasion and that locked room was the best bet he had to survive. What good was a nail gun when he would die if he did not get out of there within the next few minutes?

Croatoa knelt down next to the heavy steel table. He raised the nail gun over his head and brought the heavy piece of machinery down as hard as he could on the rusted bolts attached to the floor. The bolt cracked. It was enough to give him courage. He hammered down on it until it cracked and he ripped it out of the floor. Croatoa kept glancing out the window at the ominous body of the relentless shark. He kept checking his air every few seconds out of fear that more time passed than he anticipated. He only needed to remove three of the bolts. The nail gun was cracked. He threw it aside and pushed the heavy table so that it turned around the last bolt.

Croatoa knocked on the wall again. He administered a line of taps, listening to changes in the sounds returning to him. There were three hollow raps centered behind where the table was placed. Croatoa picked up the nail gun once more and started wildly bashing against the false wall with all of his strength. His body was exhausted, but there was so much adrenaline pumping through him because of fear that he hardly noticed the amount of pain he was in.

The wood behind the plaster and peeling paint splintered away. Croatoa kicked at it and used the nail gun to break away more and more pieces until he could peer inside. He waved his blue light into the room. It was a hoarder's haven. He could not believe his luck. There were weapons. Whether they worked or not was a whole other story. There were also all kinds of survival gear.

A lot of good all this did for the bloke.

Croatoa thought to himself as he stepped through the broken door. He moved as quick as he could, searching the items for everything that could help him distract the shark and survive the terrible event. His air was almost out. He had mere minutes to beat the shark and make it back up to the surface. Of all the things inside of the room, the firearms were ruined by algae and rust, everything else mostly dissolved and eaten away, as the room had seemingly not been air or water tight. Croatoa chose a crossbow to arm himself with, the taunt line being one of rubber encased cable, preventing it from dissolving or rusting out after so long in the cold dark water. The other item Croatoa was thankful to find was a self-inflating survival raft, one of the few items actually designed for prolonged exposure. It was one of the gigantic hexagon ones used on airplanes back in the day. He touched the folded boat with tender gratitude, geared up, and turned to face the shark.

The shark sensed Croatoa's approach with sharp movements. He ceased bashing himself against the window and lined his big black eye with the window pane to watch Croatoa. Croatoa released a bolt from the crossbow. The shark tried to move but the bolt hit him in the face, injuring him, but far from a kill shot.

The monster pulled up and began to shake side to side, trying to break the bolt free from his face. Croatoa went as fast as he could. He quickly tethered a line from the bolt to the raft, rigging it so it would inflate upon being shaken by the shark. He took deep breaths as he cautiously aimed. There was a surreal pause following the bow's release. He watched it sink into the flesh of the shark. The shark reacted violently. The chord triggered, and the large, yellow raft expanded, dragging the shark along with it.

The shark's eyes expanded and an evil essence seemed to bloom inside. Croatoa's heart rattled at such a high speed compared to his breaths as the shark was yanked up and away from the crabber. He pushed himself through the window, not knowing how fast the shark could move. Croatoa swam as hard as he could. He did not look back, too scared that it would be his end.

23.

Bard opened his eyes. The water was gray and hazy as if he was seeing it through a film. With every breath there was pain in his ribs, his mind dazed from the impact. He tried to focus, to understand what had happened. Where everyone was.

A shadowy streak passed back and forth in a small reflection of light bouncing off the walls of an apartment building across the street but he couldn't seem to make sense of everything. There was a peace to this, being unaware of the dangers all around, even if it was only for a second. Gradually his eyes finally followed the steep, brick incline up above where a shark was thrashing in front of a window, apparently fighting against the pull of a yellow life raft that was somehow attached to it.

The sight of Croatoa climbing out of the window brought everything back with a jolt.

Galvanized into action by seeing the shark doing it's best to get to Croatoa, Bard struggled to his feet and forced himself to move through water that felt like molasses around him. Every kick and stroke was an explosion of pain in his ribs and head.

Croatoa was obviously trying to get to the surface but the furious shark, despite the drag of the raft, was gaining on him.

Bard tried to swim toward them, keeping his arm reached out towards Croatoa's. Pushing his body as hard as he could, he only had a few more feet to go. Croatoa's eyes met Bard's as the shark opened its mouth Croatoa's lower body disappeared into its jaws.

Bard yelled impotently inside his helmet.

Shaking it's head back and forth, then finally satisfied with the revenge he'd inflicted, the shark released Croatoa and ceased resisting the pull of the life raft drawing the creature up to the surface.

Croatoa's body floated down in an orb of green light radiating from his forearm. His lower half was a mangled mess. Bard caught Croatoa as his body drifted down and cradled him in his arms as they sank to the sea floor. Croatoa looked at Bard, managing to grip one of Bard's arm lightly, then the life slipped from his eyes, and his body relaxed against Bard.

Shameless tears clouded his eyes as Bard sat there. Croatoa was dead. He had to say goodbye but he didn't want to leave his friend behind. He wanted to return home with his dear companion and fellow whaler. To laugh together and swap stories. Time passed for a while until Bard noticed the small line on his air gauge showed him how little time was left. The realization snapped Bard out of his fugue. No one would know how Croatoa lived or how he died if he did not survive.

He sobbed during the entire ascent to the surface, sorrow overtaking thoughts about the war raging above. Sailor Dave had yet to reappear, and since a building had not collapsed in time with the explosion, Bard suspected that the simple whaler had somehow gotten the bombs out of the building before they went off. Was he indeed the last man alive from Croatoa's entire team? This was not the first time Bard had emerged from a nightmare scenario as the last man standing, and the thought of doing so again exhausted him with survivor's guilt. It was not until he broke the surface and saw the red glow of fire shimmer through the waters far did he remember this was not the time to mourn. He pulled off his helmet and, looking around for evidence of the shark, hoping it was trapped in Seattle's canals somewhere but there was no sign of it or the raft or was attached to.

He stayed as low as he could in the water, trying to stay concealed until he assessed the surroundings. The waters were not as rough as open water, shielded by Seattle, but it sloshed and bobbed between the docks from the motion of the battle. The cries of men and women under attack in the distance echoed between buildings and over waves. There appeared to be no one in the immediate vicinity though.

Ears straining for any sign of danger, he turned slowly in the water three more times, checking and double checking the surrounding homes, businesses, and alley ways all around. When he was sure there was no one watching, he reached a hand out to a float tank covered in fishing net. The first attempt at pulling himself up was a failure as pain surged from his ribs and he buried a cry against his forearm.

The second attempt was almost a failure. The pain hit like before, but this time he was ready for it. Teeth clenched and breath sawing out in a long groan, he forced his body to drag itself up the netting and onto the floating structures connecting the city. He lay there, breath wheezing in and out in heavy pants. After a moment he looked around. There was still no one.

There was no way he would make it if he didn't get rid of the heavy diving gear. He was too weak to stand. Another glance around and he noticed a tiny shop behind him with the door was left open. It was easy to see that the Panzer Fish already swept this area for goods, no doubt right before they planned to blow it up. He managed to crawl backwards to the store, keeping an eye peeled for anyone.

It was a relief no one was inside, but the shop was in chaos. It appeared to be an apothecary set up. Books and papers fluttered in the breeze flowing in off the water. The air smelled of exotic herbs, thrown everywhere when the Panzer's had pilfered through for hidden gold and family heirlooms. As soon as he was completely inside he kicked the door shut.

He lay still, looking up at the banister lining the loft of a second floor above the shop. The smell of the ocean mingled with the pungent, sweet and spicy herbs of the shop. After a moment in the silence, Bard struggled with detaching his gear. Maybe he could stash it and eventually get it back for the *Penny Dreadful* when this was all over.

The light stick was the only thing he held on to. The effort of removing the gear had exhausted him. His body was stiff and in immense amounts of pain. The effort of the mission in the depths below had been exhausting even without the injuries he'd sustained.

As the time passed, he became aware of a new sound. It was faint and at first and he thought it must be something carried in on the wind or maybe one of those tricks silence and fear play on the mind. He tried to be more alert and strained to hear into the darkness.

Sure enough, after a long enough time of remaining still and quite, the noise came again of someone or something shuffling their position in the loft above.

"Who's there?" He called out. Not a scream. Not a whisper. Just loud enough to be heard.

Complete silence was the response.

"I heard you up there!" He said louder, when the sound came again.

It was not a Panzer Fish. A Panzer Fish would have rushed down and ended him the moment he'd crawled through the threshold. A Panzer Fish, if injured enough not to be able to kill him, would have at least thrown insults at him, egging Bard on until Bard killed him.

"I'm not going to hurt you," Bard said. "I'm actually hurt pretty bad, myself. If you're the owner of this shop, please, I need your help."

The shuffling sounds brushed against the floor boards above. After a couple minutes, the creak of old wood was accompanied by a small face peeking through the banister columns. It was a young girl. She looked about ten years old. Bard's heart sank, she was young, too young to be of help.

"Will you hurt me?" Her voice was timid and frightened.

"No," I cringed at a stab of pain in his side. "No, I won't."

"What's wrong with you?" She asked, standing up and approaching the ladder-well leading down.

"Broken ribs, I think."

The child came down a step and paused. She moved hesitantly down two more and looked at him, trying to observe more and more in the light. "Do you have any weapons?" she asked midway down.

"No," I said.

The young girl made the final passage down and hugged the perimeter of the room as she walked around me to the small drawers spilling out herbs and poultices. Her tiny hands floated above the drawers as she read each label. The labels were written in an unfamiliar language. By tilting his head as far back as he could, he could just see her. He didn't miss her slip a dagger into her skirts from one of the shelves.

The little girl, so meek before, walked with a more confident gait. Her expression was stern, as if she knew exactly what she was doing. The girl laid ingredients alongside Bard. There was a brass bowl lying upside down on a pile of loose paper. She picked it up and ran to the door.

"Stop," Bard called out. He tried to sit up and was slammed back to the floor boards, coughing.

The child looked back at him but said nothing. She opened the door a small crack and looked outside before running out. Within seconds she was back, closing the door with a slam. She had filled the bowl with sea water. The child knelt down next to Bard.

"Do you have any religious preferences?" she asked.

The question caught Bard off-guard. "N-no."

She nodded in response. "Remove your shirt."

He obeyed without question, but she ended up having to help him as the effort was almost too much . The skin stretching over my ribs was already black. The child's touch made him cry out in pain.

She poured the herbs into the sea water. Under her breath, she began chanting, her words strange and meaningless. A rich and comforting perfume filled the room. The child dipped strips of cloth into the potion and draped them gently over any visible wounds.

The cloth seared anywhere the skin was broken. Bard groaned and gasped as the salt cleansed the open wounds.

"Are there any more wounds?"

She helped him move about to reveal all of his various wounds. The places she bandaged first felt better and better as she worked her way through covering every indicated place with compresses. When the process was finished the child stood up. As he tried to move he was pressed back to the floor by the flat of the little girl's palm. Lying back he watched with curiosity as she retrieved multiple candles of different shapes and sizes from behind the counter.

The girl placed the candles in a circle around him. She then sprinkled salt in a steady stream around him until he was fully encircled by the two. She set the last of the supplies back on the counter.

She turned to me, and in total seriousness said, "If I heal you, you will be stronger than you were before. If I heal you, I need you to promise me you will get me to safety."

Bard stared at her. She was small and weak. "I can't promise I can protect you. Look at how I protected myself."

The girl turned on him, more fierce and stern than before. "Promise me you will try your hardest to see me safely through this war, and I will heal you."

Her demeanor was almost frightening even if she was just a child. Bard was puzzled and did not believe she could do more than she already had but found himself saying, "I will protect you through this war, but after the Panzer Fish are gone, you will be on your own." He thought about Artisema. There was no room for another child on board. Drucilla had a soft spot for orphans, since she, herself, was one, but they had no need for another.

The child opened up the front door and all the windows in the room. At his protest, the girl gestured for me to remain silent. The wind whipped through, and as it did the candles lit all at once without any flame bending down to their wicks.

Bard was awestruck. There were tales from all over the world about magic, but he had never believed them. They were always tales of tales of tales and wrapped in the same mystic hyperboles as so many other myths.

The girl stood beside him, outside of the circle. She pressed her palms together and her eyes shut in deep concentration, her brow knit together. After a moment in the silence and breeze, she started to walk around him, eyes closed, hands set for prayer. Bard feared she would trip into one of the brightly blazing candles, but dared not break her trance unless it was of dire necessity. After she completed the circle around him, she crouched down by his ankles, her hand hovering inches above his body. She stepped, foot over foot, awkwardly as her hand steadily glided over him.

Amazement and wonder overwhelmed him as he could feel the magic working through him and the pain lift as her hand passed over. Her hand trembled as she passed over the more injured parts of his body. When she squatted right next to his head, she jetted out both of her hands. Energy flowed from her and he could feel it. And he could feel energy being pulled from him. The exchange created a relaxed feeling and in a state of focused calm. Suddenly, the child fell back, the candles extinguished themselves and the front door slammed shut with enough force to rattle the small shack of a shop around it.

"Are you okay?" Bard asked, wondering if she'd slipped him hallucinogens in the process of patching him up, there was no way he could be feeling so much better so soon.

"Hm?" she muttered, looking around, "Yes, yes, I'm fine." She stood back up.

"Can I get up now?"

"Yeah, let me know if it worked."

Bard was skeptical, hesitant about moving, afraid the pain would wipe him back out and crush any hope of recovery. To his great surprise, not only was the pain gone, but he *did* feel stronger than before.

"Have you never done this before?" he asked, turning his hands over in amazement.

The child blushed. "I've seen my mother do it." Then the flush of tragedy rose in the girls cheeks and wet her eyes.

"How do you want to go about this," he asked, wanting to make good on his deal.

Her eyes softened.

"Do you think you can run?" She asked.

"Yes, but we need weapons."

"I know where to go near here. Until then," the child pulled a knife from inside of her pocket and passed it over his shoulder.

Bard took the knife and as he did the girl's fingers grazed his.

"My name is Lyla."

24.

Outside of the small, dilapidated apothecary shop, darkness still reigned over all of Seattle. It was dawn, yet no light penetrated the thick black smoke of war. With the sulfur mingled the smells of the dead and dying on the docks and in the churning waters of the bay.

Compared to the chaos before, the city was much quieter. The screams of war did not echo down the alleys between the various sized structures floating around the supporting skyscrapers poking over the turbulent waters. Ships still discharged their weapons from time to time, and there was still the faint clash of steel in the distance. The war cries of Panzer Fish and Seattle natives could still be heard, but the change in noise levels left an ominous feeling hovering over the entire city. It meant that the battle was mostly won or lost, the only mystery to untangle now was who would emerge the victor.

"It's going to be to your right, three doors down, Ol' Jim was a crackpot and has an arsenal hidden up in there."

"Yeah, and how do you know him or someone else hasn't cleaned it out yet?"

"I don't," Lyla said, "Do you have any better ideas?"

Bard raised his hand up in consent. Trying to conserve energy, he walked silently through the shadows cast by the small courtyard of netting, catwalks, and makeshift planks connecting the various buildings. The house she referred to was smaller than Lyla's apothecary shop. It was a shack composed of rotting, sea-stained boards and the force of the wind over too many years without repair caused it to lean heavily to one side.

The entrance to the shanty was a door with the top half able to move independently of the bottom. Crude, peeling blue block letters spelled out BAIT above it.

"He could still be in there," Lyla whispered to Bard.

Bard knocked softly on the threshold of the door. No one answered. No one stirred. He slowly pushed on it and it swung inward with a loud creaking moan. A bullet ripple through the air, close to where Bard's arm had just been and he fell back out of the way as a voice barked.

"I'm warnin' you damn fish lovers, you take one step in here an' I'll blow you to damned bits."

Lyla's voice was soft and gentle, "Jim, it's me."

"Who?" He yelled into the wind.

Bard whispered to Lyla, "Get him to stop yelling."

"I can't, he doesn't hear well," Lyla replied, panicked at the command. "Lyla, from next door!" She said louder than before.

"Who's with ya?"

"A man who saved my life. We need weapons."

"You can't stay here!" Jim yelled.

"We just need protection. We won't stay," Lyla promised. They pressed to the wall outside of the door, trying to keep out of Jim's line of fire.

The floor boards creaked under the slow step of the man approaching. A scraggly bearded head popped out. White sporadic tufts of hair sprouted from a sun spotted old head. He looked at Bard first, keeping his silenced gun trained on the center of his body. Then he looked Lyla over who gave him a sweet smile.

"Had to be sure it was you, Lassie. Get 'n here 'fore they see you."

There were no windows in the shack. There was bait and bits for fishing and what not, a moth eaten cot, a sturdy handmade table, and the rest of the room was devoted to guns and ammunition. The Panzer Fish must have over looked the shanty as useless and a waste of time, but in reality it was a full arsenal comparable to that of the entire *Penny Dreadful*.

"I can't spare much, got ten times more guns than bullets ya know. Don' know what's comin' yet an' all. An' you better give 'em back to me when this is all done." The old man gave the little girl an assault rifle and a small satchel filled with ammunition. "You know how to use it, right?" He spit a wad of tobacco out on the planks of his floor.

Lyla shook her head, 'no.' Jim did not say anything. He showed her what to do to load it, unloaded it, had her do it herself, showed her how to jam the magazine and reload it when it was empty. She tried to press the bullets into the magazine. They would not pop in like when he did it. She pressed as hard as she could.

"No, try it like this, more pressure up here," he showed her again.

Her weak, soft fingers trembled as she did as he said. To her satisfaction the bullet clicked in. The next ones were easier, and soon she loaded her first magazine all by herself. Her hands trembled slightly as she held the automatic rifle.

"Don't be scared, missy, jus' keep that barrel pointed down til' you're ready to shoot," The old man walked around and stared at me, "An' what's your excuse. Why the fuck ain't you armed, boy?"

Lyla spoke for me, "He was injured pretty bad when I got him. He came in on the *Penny Dreadful*."

Bard stared at her, shocked. He had never told her that.

The man eyed him suspiciously, but gave him the same weapon as Lyla's as well as a couple pistols to attach to his side. "Lyla, these are comin' back to me or you'll be workin' for 'em for a long time, understand?"

"Yes, sir."

"Alright, now get the fuck outta my house before you give away my position. If you die out there, I'm takin' your shit as payment, Lyla. Where your parents anyhow?"

Lyla's face darkened, "Not sure just yet, Jim. Hopin' they show up back here later when this is all done."

"Well," Jim dropped eye contact from the girl, "Take care of that an' get as many of those fuckers as you can. This man seems strong enough to protect you an' if he don't I'll come for him."

There were no goodbyes. Jim looked both ways outside of his door before allowing them to exit, then slammed it shut behind them. They could hear him walk back to whatever point in the shack he was keeping guard, and then that same odd silence greeted us once more. This portion of the city already saw its worst of the battle. All of the action was taking place closer to the bay.

25.

"What's the plan?" Lyla asked.

"Shh. Keep your voice down," Bard snapped, "I have a lancing boat hidden away not too far from here, where we first dove down. If it is still there, that's our best bet. We need to get to my ship." He stayed crouched and alert, "Keep an eye on our back, Lyla, I need to be able to trust you."

"You can, I promise."

Every time they approached the cross section of an alley or turned onto a new street, Bard paused to make a full observation of the area. Where he looked the gun was pointed, first checking down one way, down the other, and then sweeping the buildings above for signs of movement. It was a quarter of a mile to get to the lancing boats. he hoped to avoid most of the action on the bay front. If it had just been him, he would charge through them with guns blazing in the name of vengeance. The child at his back made him want to avoid anyone. Not that he was all that good with firearms anyway, rare as they were he'd not used them much, and found it somewhat frustrating that the old man had hoarded such firepower instead of deploying it in defense of the city.

For two-thirds of the blocks, they did not hear another soul. Finally, Bard could see the point where the boat had been moored. They'd done a good job of hiding it in the shadows but had not thought of the possibility of being ambushed on land, only of remaining invisible. Bard slowed down as he approached the dead end.

It was the perfect position for sniping and the sounds of battle were closer. They were only a few streets down, parallel to the main chaos. Bard swept the area with the rifle, paranoid that in the darkness they would meet enemy fire.

Blat. Blat. Blat. Blat.

The unexpected impact of Lyla's blasts from behind caused him to stumble forward. Lyla's rifle fired off more rounds. Bard took a deep breath, and sprinted for the lancing boat.

It was gone.

"*Fuck!*" Bard snarled. "Did you get 'em, Lyla?" He ran behind a brick wall for cover.

Her voice shook, "I-I think so," He could hear her quick breaths, "My hands won't stop shaking, Bard."

"Breathe deep, girl, I need your head in the game. If we don't kill them, they'll kill us. They'll kill your parents and they'll kill ol' Jim. They'll do worse things even. How many of them did you see?"

"I-I don't know. Eight—nine, maybe."

"And their weapons? Did they have guns."

"One of them, but he didn't shoot at us."

"He might not have ammo. Okay, here's the thing, we have ammo, Lyla. We can do this. Now, my boat is gone which means we need to make it to the bay front. My ship will help us get back on board if they see us. There will be other vessels we can take if we have to."

The sounds of the Panzer Fish's boots were close by. They could hear them beating the decks towards us.

Bard lowered his voice to a whisper. "We have the advantage. At least with this group. Deepen your breaths and your hands will steady. Remember, if you steady those hands, your gun can wipe out all of them, but when it runs empty that's pretty much it. More people than bullets left in this world. Can you see alright?"

"Yeah, I can."

"Are you ready?"

"N-no," she muttered.

Bard looked up. The men would turn around the corner any second. Above him was a rusty ladder well. The first rung was quite a bit above his head, but he took a gamble and jumped. The amount of strength Lyla's treatment had given him was astonishing. Maybe she'd dosed him with methamphetamine. They made it to the rooftop just as the Panzer Fish turned the corner to attack them. Lyla's gun went off again. The machine gun's rattle echoed off the walls of the alley ways.

"That's my girl! Anyone left?"

"No," He could hear the adrenaline rush in her voice, feel it pulsating off of her, "Gun's empty now though."

"Ditch it, we need to move fast. The old man can bill me for it. They're gonna come for us now. Game plan: we stick to narrow alleys. Remember to scan the roof tops. Archers could be anywhere."

"Why don't we stay up here?" she asked as he leaped between the small gap dividing two buildings.

"Hmph. Cause, we'll get stuck eventually at the port."

Thankfully, much of their journey continued without incident.

Suddenly the tormented screams of a woman came to them. Bard tried to turn down an alley way to avoid it.

"Bard! No! We have to help her! Oh please, help her!" Lyla begged.

"Aaaaghhh," he groaned, "Lyla we have to keep moiving or we're not gonna make it! Maybe it's a trap!"

"Please, I don't care, just help her. I can't stand the sounds of those cries."

He could hear Lyla crying. She might act like a miniature adult but she was still a child. Kicking himself for his own stupidity, he cursed loudly and began running towards the sound of the woman screaming. "You better have my back!" he whispered harshly over his shoulder.

"I promise!" she said.

When he got there he was grateful Lyla was faced away. Two Panzer fish were taking turns with the woman, her clothes were torn to shreds, her body bloody and bruised, her face battered, yet she still struggled against her attackers.

Bard drew his pistol as he engaged them at point blank range, not at all confident in his aim. The corpses of the two cultists fell as he pumped rounds into their necks and head. The woman screamed and shoved the one who'd been raping her off and pulled herself away, weeping.

A cultist jumped from the roof next to them and struck Bard across the back of the head with a blunt object. Hoots and warcries sounded in the alleys and rooftops around them. They were surrounded.

The Panzer Fish attacked with a crowbar. Bard recovered in time to dodge the swing and grab the Panzer Fish by the collar of his hodge-podge armor and headbutted him three times. When the cultist fell back his face was a mangled mess.

"Pick that pistol up and grieve later, dammit." Bard yelled at the injured woman as he tossed her his other pistol.

The woman seemed to come back to herself. She up the gun, and got shakily to her feet. One of her breasts was bare and bore the cuts of a blade across them, her clothes were in shreds and blood dripped down her legs turning her feet black. Her eyes became wild raised the gun and began to fire. Her hands did not shake and her aim was deadly. One, two, three Panzer Fish fell dead around them.

There was a click as the woman's gun came up empty. One of the cultists ran as fast as he could toward them, his bludgeon raised above his head, no doubt hoping to cave in Lyla's skull.

Bard emptied his magazine at the cultist, not trusting his aim to be as crisp, and his fullisade ripped the attacker to bits. Blood splattered all over Lyla and the woman as their would be attacker he fell to his knees and died merely a foot in front of them.

26.

Aboard the *Penny Dreadful* hope was thin and everyone was exhausted. The other massive whaling vessels had undergone so much fire and pressure from the enemy before the *Penny* even arrived, they were useless or sunk now. Their stores of ammunition were spent, and the one still still sailing was more focused on trying to save itself than re-engaging the Panzer Fish. The entire battlefield was still swarming with sharks, though their numbers were dramatically reduced, and while the Panzer Fish had died in droves and no longer had the upper hand, they too continued to attack in small gangs. It had become a war of attrition and sheer endurance, and while the enemy attack was all but spent, it appeared that for the remaining cultists any carnage was good carnage.

Artisema's eyes were heavy. Vladimir could see how exhausted she grew. If there was a lull even for a second in command or action, her eyes would slip shut and her head would nod, only to bounce back up in fear.

"It vill end soon, little one." Vlad assured her. "Stand up an' be strong."

She swayed back and forth. Catching her before she fell completely unconscious, Vlad lowered her to a crate to sit on. Aboard the *Penny*, they had sustained seven deaths to arrow, shark, or blade, in addition to the loss of everyone who had followed Riddle aboard the crab boat. Kalak and the sharkers had rode straight into the swarm and disappeared in the darkness and chaos. The rest of the crew now threatened to fall simply from exhaustion.

"What's that?" Artisema was wide awake now. She pointed to a mass on the docks.

Vladimir laughed and bounced on the balls of his feet in excitement. "Not a Panzer! Look at him go!"

They watched as a gang of cultists emerged from a building, fleeing from something, and only to be cut down to a man as someone inside the building began rapid firing some kind of firearm. The cultists did not stand a chance, and in the blink of an eye five of them were dead on the ground.

Drucilla appeared alongside Mr. Pit, her face flushed from running. She left the wheel to the deckhand. Like a flash of lightening, her spyglass snapped open as sudden as a spark. Artisema jumped at the flash of the metal accompanied by the rapid clicks appearing in her peripherals.

"*It's Bard!*" breathed Drucilla.

"What's he carrying?" One of the female archers pressed herself against the railing.

Drucilla squinted through her spyglass. "It looks like a pre-Melt machine gun." She replied in surprise.

The joy at seeing one of their comrades decimating the Panzer Fish on the shores of Seattle renewed the ship's spirits. All at once they noticed things were not as dreary as they seemed under the blanket of fatigue and hopelessness. The fires of Seattle were dwindling and late morning forced itself through the smog in thin weak patches. It would not be long until the sun shone upon them. They could hold on for awhile longer. There were still arrows in their fists and blades on their hips.

Before, the sheer forces secured within the city walls frightened them most. No matter how much effort they had poured in, every time they looked up and saw the cultists invading, their hearts broke. They were helpless to the people within those walls. They could only destroy those few on the docks.

Bard's appearance, while of little tactical significance, was the morale boost they needed to carry the day. Their efforts doubled as they saw him wipe out another gang of the Panzers within seconds. Few had seen pre-Melt weapons in action, and it was as loud as it was impressive. Drucilla commanded her ship to get as close to the docks as she could without risking grounding themselves. The Captain knew from her father that such weapons might be a wonder, but they ran out of ammunition quickly, and they needed to turn the tide before Bard went empty.

Her presence among her crew strengthened them. "Now is the time to fight! All is futile if we lose now! There will be no tomorrow if we do not fight with every ounce of strength we have. We are warriors of the sea, and our enemies will not defeat us!"

Drucilla let out a battle cry, jabbing her cutlass to the sky as the crew took up the horrific scream and leapt over the side and onto the docks.

The cultists on the dock realized they could rush the man with the gun or fight the skirmishers surging out of the whaleship, and decided to take their changes in the melee as the two forces collided.

Beyond them, in the bay, Kalak and one surviving sharker rode their jet skis out of the darkness to engage the sharks swarming at the base of the docks.

As Bard drove the enemy before him with punishing fire from the ancient weapon, Drucilla and Mr. Pit led their skirmishers to cut a bloody swathe through the remaining cultists.

Once the last cultist fell it was as if a spell binding the sharks to the frenzied warriors was broken, and as it was in Blue Stone, when the final Panzers on the docks fell and those still on the water fled, the shark swarm broke and swam for the open ocean.

Within moments the crew were back on the *Penny Dreadful* as Drucilla ordered a pursuit. Every shark they killed today was one less they'd face later, and she knew that once her people took a moment to relax they'd all crash.

"Your strength will wane soon," the child spoke softly in Bard's ear.

Bard nodded, he had felt it sinking it for a while now. The empty gun grew heavier by the moment. It took most of his strength to pull the both of them over the side of the *Penny Dreadful* despite the willing hands helping them. Once he made it over, he fell hard to one knee beneath the weight. Lyla rushed to aid him.

Drucilla was the first to arrive beside him. She created a protective barrier from the crew. "Everyone back to positions! We've sharks to kill!" The archers returned to their posts, temporarily distracted by Bard's appearance. "Where is Croatoa?" she demanded.

Bard pursed his lips and shook his head. Drucilla's stiffened, her face falling. Bard gestured for her spyglass. "Can I see that?"

Drucilla handed it over. She stood behind Bard as he scanned the horizon, sweeping back and forth, *"There's the fucker!"* He shoved the spyglass back at Drucilla.

Drucilla looked through the glass where Bard directed and saw a shark with a yellow life raft dragging behind it trying to evade Kalak, who was already in hot pursuit. The raft was losing air, but it still created enough drag through the water it slowed the beast down.

27.

The crew's spirits became fired up as Bard shared the news of the dive teams' death. The deckhands mourned Sailor Dave, along with Tak, Chimp, and the others, though like they had for Morgan the entire ship demanded blood for Croatoa's death. There were hardly any Panzer Fish left. The ones who managed to get a hold of a jet ski or boat had taken off, away from the battlefield. Though once Bard pointed out the giant shark dragging the raft, the crew's vengeance had a target.

Drucilla brought the ship right onto the back of the shark that killed Croatoa. It was a smart monster, and saw the *Penny Dreadful* zeroing in on it. Bard tried to lift a harpoon to throw it, but had gone too weak, and reluctantly handed the weapon to Abigail. Before the warrior could throw it Captain Drucilla lashed a line and rescue bouy to it, and then nodded for Abigail to make her throw. The expert warrior launched the harpoon towards the beast and it sank into the shark's back with a sickening thud. The shark bucked against it, attempting to free himself from the harpoon's grasp.

Abigail lodged the harpoon between the railings and a plate of armor protruding from the ship's hull even as she and Mr. Pit held the shaft steady to keep it from snapping like a fishing pole. The shark pulled with all of its might but it wasn't until the ship's railing groaned that he cut the line. The rope snapped back to the Shark, lashing a clean pink strip through its back. The shark kept swimming, and yet it did not have the strength to dive.

"Mr. Pit have Rover keep sights on the beast! It can't dive thanks to the raft and bouy, we'll follow it home and finish this." Drucilla shouted to her first mate, "Get Kalak and any of the sharkers who survived aboard. Dispatch a runner to the other whaleship, it looks like the *Meridian*. Get them to join pursuit long enough to broadside with the *Penny*, we need fresh crew and more supplies, and I figure they owe us at least that before we let them rest."

The crew exalted in Drucilla's decision with cheers. They were exhausted but the thought of ending the battle once and for all, awakened the fury inside of them.

The rest of the shark swarm fled faster and deeper than the injured shark attached to the raft, and by the time the *Meridian* had willingly given over eight seasoned whalers, two sharkers, and what they could spare of fresh water, food, oil, and arrows, there was but the single monster swimming ahead of the whaleship.

"It looks like he's headed for the Cascadian Sea."

Bard was in the wheel house with Drucilla and Abigail, charting the trajectory of the swarm and the injured shark.

"There's a reef here," Abigail placed her finger on a reef on the south border of the Sea.

"I bet that's where the bastards have been spawning," Drucilla spit inside of the wheel house at the mention of them. "Bard."

"Yes, Captain."

"Mr. Pit has his hands full integrating the new crew and re-supply, give him a hand won't you? Do you still have ammunition for that pre-Melt gun?"

"One magazine Captain," He looked up at Drucilla.

"Good, this ends tonight. Rotate men out every four hours, everyone needs at least one sleep shift before we hit the reef, am I clear?"

"Aye, Captain." Bard nodded, exhausted but ready for action.

"I need you to sleep too, Abigail." Drucilla said.

"And what about you?" Abigail crossed her arms over her chest.

Drucilla sighed and rubbed her brows, "If we're right about this, we should be there within ten hours, twelve if the winds turn against us. That gives everyone a small time to sleep. I need my crew in top shape."

"And we need our captain in the same. Look," Abigail placed her hand on the helm, "You know I can do this. Sleep six hours.

I'll sleep four, and you'll be able to get full rest right before we arrive."

Drucilla looked at Abigail warily. She didn't like the idea of being one of the first to sleep. Abigail had spoken wisely though. If she did not get enough rest, she would be useless by the time they reached the reef. Drucilla rotated her chair around and stood up. She gestured with a small bow for Abigail to take her seat.

"Go rest," Abigail smiled. "I've got this. I won't let that bastard get away."

"Don't let anyone shoot him either. That kill is either Bard's or mine, understood?"

"Yes, ma'am."

No one argued with Drucilla's orders. Mr. Pit took volunteers for the first set of people on watch. Most of the ship wasn't needed. The wind was just right which meant the *Penny Dreadful* flew her brightly colored, silk sails and saved the rest of the whale oil for pushing engine back to Seattle against the wind.

Bard spent some time looking for Lyla after leaving a message with Mr. Pit. He found her in the berthing healing all the crew members. When he approached her, she ignored him completely until she was done binding a man's leg where an arrow had cut through him.

"Do you have more medical supplies?" the girl asked.

"I would ask Vladimir if I were you," at her look of confusion, he added, "Tall guy with the black skull cap up there, thick accent, you can't miss him."

She nodded, "And, when all of this is over, you will make sure I get back to Seattle with those guns, right?"

Bard laughed, "Yes, we're not holding you captive."

"Well, I don't think I'm supposed to be here."

Bard looked around the compartment they were standing in. There were racks of people wrapped in the same muslin gauze Lyla held in her hands. She let out a small huff of impatience and pushed past him.

"I think you should get some sleep, Lyla, there are plenty of empty bunks after the few weeks we've had." His face fell as he thought about the people who used to occupy those bunks. "And there is another girl about your age around here too, Artisema."

Lyla continued to walk towards the ladder well leading to above decks. He went after her. "Seriously," he said, "You need sleep like everyone else."

Lyla turned on him. She was a gentle creature, but something inside of her stirred just then. "Your people need my help right now. When I have cleaned everyone's wounds and made sure they are properly bandaged, I will go to sleep, and I will stay asleep until I am needed to clean up the next battle. Does that work for you, Bard?"

"Well," slightly dazed by her sharp tongue, he mumbled, "Yeah."

"Good, now take me to this Vladimir guy."

28.

It was the middle of the night when everyone on board the *Penny Dreadful* was woken up from their brief chance at sleep. The shark they followed had slowed considerably compared to the fierceness it displayed hours ago and the yellow raft floated along on the surface with the small bouy, moving in jerks.

"How much further do you think we have?" Abigail asked Kalak.

"See that line," Kalak pointed out a line where the water glowed the soft phosphorescent hues of blue and pink.

"Yeah," she replied.

"That's the reef. We should be there soon."

The *Penny Dreadful*'s sails were taken in. Drucilla wanted them to be ghosts upon the water and she feared getting too close to the reef's barrier and wrecking her ship on it. The captain ordered for the ship to be anchored there in the bay. Members of the crew lined the rails watched the reflective yellow of the life raft disappear past the reef.

The entire ship mustered above decks. The only two people missing were Lyla and Artisema. The girls slept soundly down below in the berthing.

"We have all fought long and hard, only to sail like madmen on half-sleep to this reef. We have lost many of those who are dear to us because of these Panzer Fish. The sharks have hurt our hunting grounds as well as the villages we come from and trade with. Tonight, we kill them all." The men and women pressing near Drucilla raised their fists and shook them in a silent cheer. "I am hoping we catch the cultists off guard. I am hoping they will be surprised and tired from journeying so far after such a large battle. The goal is to herd them all together and slaughter them here and now. We use sharkers to corral them and lancers to do the butcher's work."

Drucilla did not need to tell her people what was to be done. Everyone split into their separate units and prepared whatever weapons they favored.

The small units disembarked into the darkness from the ship. Drucilla kept her spyglass on them and could faintly make out the outlines of each lancing boat and jet ski. The moon was bright above. All was silent except the wind whistling over the waves, and the sound of the oars cutting through the waters.

The first signs of human life were lights illuminating the waters. They were dim and the light fought to penetrate a thick layer of grime accumulated on them from being exposed to the weather over the years. Drucilla counted eight of them and assumed there must be sixteen people on watch over the length of the reef. She motioned for everyone to split up. The lancing boats and jet skis all approached different areas.

Kalak and Mr. Pit were both on jet skis. They decided they would loop completely around the reef. On the back side of the reef there were only two lights watching the ocean. This was probably because there were few settlements on that side of the reef.

Kalak smiled as he looked at the weapon Vladimir blessed him with. It was a nail gun modified to be a sniper rifle, complete with a silencer, so no muzzle flash. He set it up on the top of his handlebars, thankful the ocean was so calm. Through the sights, he could see the watchmen. It was even better than they expected. There was only one person standing watch per light. Within seconds, Kalak's rifle fired and the watchmen began to fall where they stood. Other sharkers hurled spears and fired compact bows, and soon all that guarded the bay were dead men and lanterns.

No one came immediately to help the watchmen. No one alerted anyone. The Panzer Fish were not prepared for anyone to attack them, so far was the thought from their mind that anyone would be so daring. It did look, however, as if someone on the parts of the reef, in the shanty town that rested atop the part of the reef closest to the surface, had seen the whaleship at last. It was just as well, the whaleship could not hide forever. At least the sailors were in position.

Kalak and Mr. Pit gunned their engines and within moments both of them made it to the place the cultists kept their jet skis and smaller craft. The lancing boats were still coming in, the other sharkers on the edge of the reef would be needed to keep the sharks from escaping, and could offer no help in handling the Panzer Fish. Good thing they had a Vladimir on the crew.

As the cultists approached the jet skis they were shocked as sudden explosions erupted in front of them. If there was any intent of attacking the *Penny*, it was blunted as Mr. Pit and Kalak poured gallons of whale oil all over the vehicles and the base of the shanty town, running their jet skis across the community as they splashed oil everywhere. Mr. Pit struck a flint and the single spark sent a rush of flame across the surface of the water and into the tightly packed group of vessels and jet skis. The two men let up a cry of victory as the rest of the oil caught and some of the buildings began to catch fire. The strong ocean breeze did the rest, and in moments the fire was spreading beyond control as the cultists scrambled to either put out the fires or counter attack.

Two men with surf boards fearlessly streaked out into the bay, launching themselves from the low slung docks for Mr. Pit. Kalak sent a nail into one of their skulls. The other attempted to bring a broad sword down on Mr. Pit, which he blocked with his hammer. He continued to block one attack after another until the cultist slowed from exhaustion. With one mighty blow, Mr. Pit crushed the last offenders skull, spraying blood over the both of them. Mr. Pit let a war cry rip from his lips. His call was answered by the rest of the crew approaching the reef's shores in their long boats.

For the most part, the sharks were already at a disadvantage inside the reef. They were able to navigate the small channels in between clumps of dead coral connecting the reef, but without their cult masters to release them, they were all but trapped. Penned as they already were by the cult, which appeared to have constructed a submerged system of cages and corrals, they were easy pickings for the lancer crews. The few who managed to flip themselves over the edges of their confines were swiftly mulched by the sharkers prowling on the reef's edge. Drucilla's boat, intended as an assault craft instead of joining the lancers, was the first to join Mr. Pit upon shore as he and Kalak dismounted for the chance to fight the Panzer Fish man to man.

The Panzers fought as hard as they could. They just barely outnumbered the forces of the *Penny Dreadful*, but after the failed raid on Blue Stone and what would come to be known as the Battle of Seattle, their numbers were vastly reduced. The majority of them were injured in one way or another. Drucilla could muster an ounce of pity as her cutlass sliced through one and then another and another.

"Look!" Drucilla cried.

With the spreading fires illuminating the entire area, it became clear that the cultists and several of the sharks who were able to escape the lancer's fury were heading for a small portion of the reef in attempts to guard it. Drucilla pointed to the area. The rest of her men unloaded from the boat and joined in the battle. The cultists, seeing Drucilla point out the spot where the enemy was retreating, heightened their attacks.

"Nasty woman!" A man wearing a sea turtle's skull over his face attacked Drucilla from out of nowhere.

His blow barely missed her. She tried to hit him with her cutlass, but he deflected her blow with his steel bow staff. Small skulls decorated the staff at both ends. She couldn't tell for sure, but they looked to be the bones of small children. This angered and fueled Drucilla's attack more than ever.

"Where are all your people going, huh?" She said as she sliced her way closer to the cultist. "There's no escape, you should give up now."

He laughed, "Ha! We fight with the power of *Kaiku* in our souls!"

The man's eyes narrowed into slits. She could see the pure loathing. He tried to attack her once more and missed, his anger and his frustration clouding his judgment. Drucilla hit him with a south paw right in the jaw line before following up with an upwards assault with her cutlass. He felt the blow on his face. It stunned him. He tried to jump away from her sword, but the tip of her blade cut a clean line through his armor.

He was not critically injured, but he was slowed down. She could see the bleeding seeping over the thin armor leather he wore over his body. She pulled a long dagger from her boot in the moment he took to touch the blood on his abdomen.

He lunged forward with more fury, but Drucilla was ready. She met each of his blows. Despite being able to block, the Panzer Fish managed to push her back, one step at a time, driven by the fury of madness. Coral crumbled beneath one of her feet at the reef's edge and she felt her balance teeter.

A shark erupted from the water behind her, jaws opening wide.

29.

Drucilla was suddenly hit from the side and went tumbling into the coral, her forearms cut and scraped by the sharp bits and the salt they were coated with burning her. She looked up to see Riddle above her, dueling another attacker with a blade affixed to her mechanical arm and Bard throwing the cultist who cornered Drucilla into the hungry mouth of the shark.

The crew of the *Penny Dreadful* fought fearlessly. The Panzers were driven back. A few of the sharks lingered near them, hoping to snatch a few from the edges of the reef, however the rest escaped into the same cove so many others already retreated into.

"No quarter asked!" shouted Drucilla as she rose to her feet with sword in hand.

"None given!" answered the voices of the *Penny Dreadful.*

Blood spilled on both sides. Warriors screamed. Man, woman, and shark died by the dozen.

And then, as suddenly as it began, it was over. The only sounds being the last cries of the dying, the wet slap of bloody waves against the coral, and the crackle of the fires now consuming the modest cult settlement.

Drucilla motioned for everyone to gather near her.

"That cove is where they are all fleeing too. I bet you anything that's where their main center is. It could be the most fortified portion of the entire reef. Do you all see the ridges lining the cove?"

She pointed to the dark line cutting through the stars above the small entrance. The men all nodded, letting Drucilla know they saw what she spoke of.

"That's where we want to be. Kalak and Mr. Pit, I want you to finish running around this reef and kill anyone outside of that cove. Kill the sharks you see. Kill everything. Bard and Abigail, you will guard the entrance to the cove. Do not let anyone or anything escape. The rest of you will follow me up on that ridge."

The moon was setting over the horizon. The majority of the crew followed Drucilla up to the ridge.

The rest of the men and women followed Drucilla's orders to sneak around the ridgeline surrounding the cove. It was rough terrain, mostly composed of loose volcanic rock. There was still the cover of darkness, but it faded into the beginning shades of dawn's grey as the approached the top. The crew was prepared, armed as sunlight fell began to brighten the sky.

The first rays of dawn illuminated the jaws of what could only be a megalodon, easily one as large as the titanic beast that Captain Raj had died to slay. They were huge and hovered above a large group of tide pools.

At first Drucilla only saw the crude outlines of each pool. As the daylight grew she became aware of mass amounts of movement. At first she thought it must be reflections off the water or small marine animals. When light finally flooded in, Drucilla felt her stomach grow queasy.

The tide pools were filled with baby sharks. Thousands of them.

Drucilla and her crew kept their bellies flat to the rocky wall. She studied the landscape before her. So far it was clear that the Panzer Fish expected them to come in through the cove's entrance where the ocean pooled.

Most of the men tending the pools below, hurling chum at the multitudes of young were armed and dressed in the usual Panzer Fish attire. They were covered from head to toe with various bones all arranged to resemble the prehistoric fish after which they were named. Four of them stood huddled closest to the wall beneath the great jaws of the Megalodon. They wore long flowing, brown hooded robes. The robes were wet around the feet and wrists.

"Look at that," Riddle let out a low whistle.

Drucilla followed her gaze, "They've been branding and training them. That's what those markings mean." On the furthest side from Dru, there were two metal corrals built into the shallowest part of the main pool exiting into the ocean.

"The water is rising, Dru," Riddle said. She tore the tip off a cigar and spit the end down below, making ready the small cannon attachment she now sported for an arm, once it's up they'll flood the ocean and we'll have a whole new swarm of fully grown sharks in a few months.

30.

Drucilla raised her fist into the air to signal to her crew spread out around her. She could almost feel everyone tighten and shift into position. Sights of crossbows, projectile missiles, modified slingshots, and nail guns were among some of the weapons they carried. The dozen or so Panzer Fish who had retreated into the shark breeding shrine joined the half dozen already present, and as the rest of the whaleship's crew joined the Captain, for the numerical superiority was on the side of the sailors.

Every member of the *Penny Dreadful* was pissed. This was beyond delaying their hunting season to help their home port out. They had lost so many people. It was hard to tell who released the first shot. An arrow sliced through one of the hooded men who let out a gargled howl which echoed off all of the walls.

Riddle's hand cannon sent an explosive projectile into one of the tide pools, and when it detonated it sent hundreds of shattered shark body parts hurling into the air. The other three monk-like figures fell to their knees in grief, pulling at their hair, as they watched the small sharks pop from the water like drops of liquid on hot oil. The pools grew darker and darker with blood as they rained down upon the sharks and cultists.

Abigail and Bard, seeing that there was no escape for the Panzer Fish now, pressed into the mouth of the cove to engage the larger sharks that swam in circles. Bard pulled the pin on one of Vlad's gas grenades and tossed it. Several sharks sank to the bottom of the shallow pool as the deadly weapon wreaked havoc on their tightly packed bodies.

The sounds of weapons roaring down on the cultists mingled with the roar of the incoming tide. The sharks tried to flee from the cove and back out to sea, the larger ones chomping the smaller ones just to get ahead in their frenzy to escape. The big shark with the yellow raft still attached was the closest to the entrance but being the slowest, he clogged the exit for everybody else. Bard shouted in fury as he emptied the magazine of his pre-Melt weapon at the packed cove entrance, his hurricane of rounds tearing into the beast that killed Croatoa and mangling many other sharks alongside it.

Riddle's brows drew together until they were nearly one. Her anger erupted with the blast of her cannon across the entire cove. Mr. Pit was using his thick arms to brace her tiny body as she fired round after round into the pools. She started with the baby sharks and worked up to the humans.

The Panzer Fish had nowhere to go. Some of them jumped into the metal corrals, protected by the underwater bars and the edge of the ledge. The problem was Rover took note of them splashing into the water and clinging to the bars, shivering through the onslaught.

The deckhand kept crouched low as he repositioned himself. An arrow flew past him, causing him to fall back. He landed hard on the rough stone which cut into the flesh of his hands and arms. Instead of standing straight up, he grit his teeth and army crawled over to the edge of the bowl. He was packing a homemade shot gun.

Down below there were four men currently hiding in the corrals. They clung to the bars, soaking wet, freezing half to death. The one who shot at him had his bow and arrow awkwardly on the outside of one of the top bars. Each time a wave rolled through it bucked them against the rock walls. The shot gun sounded off.

Chk-chk. *Boom.*

The head of the Panzer with the bow and arrow exploded, a piece of his skull rocketed straight into the eye of the Panzer Fish closest to him, who let out a blood curdling scream. Brain matter covered all three of the remaining cultists.

Chk-chk. *Boom.*

One after the other, Rover made good use of the 6 shots he had, picking each one off without another shot being fired at him.

By the time the sun reached its apex in the sky, not a single being lived down below. The waters boiled a deep crimson. Some of the sharks' carcasses escaped back out to sea, but most of them piled up and clogged the cove entrance creating an organic dam. All of the small sharks floated on top of the water.

Riddle was the last to stop firing. She let a conquering scream rattle throughout her entire body.

The rest of the crew also took up triumphant hoots and hollers as they realized it was over. Abigail, Mr. Pit, Kalak, and Bard joined the jubilation on the top of the ridge. Drucilla looked down at the slaughter below.

"I want those jaws," Drucilla commanded as she stared down at the massive mouth of the Mega.

31.

It was late afternoon on the next day when the *Penny Dreadful* spotted the city of Seattle in the distance. She broke the blue water line with the dark outline of her remaining structures. Small wisps of white smoke smoldered up from the last embers of the fires from battle. Drucilla stood at the bow of the ship.

The journey home gave rest to the minds of most of the crew. It was a moment to grieve in the privacy of one's rack. It was a time to sleep and forget about the world, knowing now that they were safe from the shark swarms. As they approached Seattle, this respite ended as they faced the aftermath of so much violence. Up ahead they could hear the shouts of people finding the injured and the dead. There was work to be done.

At the aft end of the ship, Artisema looked out at deformed dolphins leaping through the wake of the vessel.

"Thank you." Riddle's voice startled the small girl.

"Oh," Artisema blushed and cast her eyes to the ground.

"I would have died if it was not for you. I thought—," Riddle swallowed her words in an attempt at composing herself. "I thought that was the end."

Riddle offered Artisema her flask. As soon as she took it, Riddle offered her the cigar from her mouth. The 13 year old took an awkward swig from the flask and a timid puff from the cigar.

Down below the decks, Abigail and Bard stole away into the empty berthing. Abigail propped a chair up against the door to bar the entrance. When she turned around, Bard was directly behind her. He slipped his hands around her sides feeling her warm skin beneath them.

Abigail leaned forward and cooed in his ear, "We were amazing."

The sound of her voice sent shivers rolling down Bard's spine. He lifted her chin and kissed her deeply. Abigail backed up under the pressure of the embrace, letting him guide her to the wall space beside the door, pinning her into place, his hands ran over her body.

Abigail let out a soft moan as he nibbled at her neck. "I can't believe we're still alive," she said.

No one disturbed them. Though the entire ship was still in mourning, a weight lifted from them as they arrived in Seattle's ports. Drucilla held no expectations for any of her crew and ensured them at least a few hours liberty before helping Seattle under obligation. The whaleship had fought hard to defend Seattle, and already the locals had brought sufficient gifts of thanks that in some ways the fighting had paid better than a hold full of leviathan kills. Half of the whalers from the *Meridian* asked to remain aboard, and took a second brand.

Kalak and Mr. Pit were the first to board lancing boats and take them onto the docks. Bodies were strewn all over the place. Most of the small structures suffered heavy damage between the main port and the center of Seattle. Everywhere the sounds of people in mourning echoed through the smoky haze. The duo immediately set to work helping the hospital and emergency response teams triage the victims.

Most of the homes that survived the fire and explosives still suffered damage from the cultists pillaging. Glass created a crystalline coat over most of the city. Kalak felt the glass bite into his knees as he knelt to tag two more bodies black for dead. Mr. Pit walked by the distinctly armored leg of a Panzer Fish, kicking it into the ocean as he passed.

Back on board the *Penny Dreadful*, Lyla waited until Bard left Abigail and returned above decks.

"Bard," she called as she saw him appear from the ladder well.

The girl looked up at him with her big brown eyes, "I just wanted to say thanks for keeping me safe."

Bard knelt down on one knee to make eye contact with her, "Thank you for saving my life."

The girl squeezed him tight. When she released him from her embrace, he stood up and asked, "Would you like me to help you home?"

Lyla looked over her shoulder before replying, "No, I've made arrangements to catch a boat to Seattle in a moment. I need to find out what happened to my parents if I can."

Bard sobered again at mention of the fallen. Croatoa's death flashed before his eyes. He Paused for a moment to reground himself. Lyla watched him, her face twisted in empathy. "I hope you find them," he said. "Do you have your friend's weapons?"

"Yes, they are already loaded."

Bard squeezed her shoulder. "Take care, Lyla. Who knows, we may cross paths again."

The girl gave a weak smile. One of the deckhands called for her attention. She turned and left, offering a small wave goodbye as she climbed into the boat.

As soon as Lyla pulled up to the docks she could see the mess Seattle was left with. There was so much blood it was difficult to discern whose body was friend and who cultists except for the armor when it was visible.

Lyla headed straight to the hospital. She kept her eyes in a thousand yard stare the entire way. If she needed to step around a corpse or heard the cries of the injured crying out to her, she zoned out and kept focused on the thought of being reunited with her family at the hospital.

The East side of the hospital was charred black from a fire started by the Panzer Fish. The rest of the building went unscathed. Even blocks away, Lyla had to avoid getting in the way of the traffic. If people were not helping the injured or moving bodies to be identified, they were preparing clean drinking water and clearing any immediate hazards.

Lyla waited inside the lobby of the ER. She dared not interrupt anybody as they slaved to save who they could. Eventually, a middle-aged man with dark salt-n-pepper hair stepped out. He pulled his mask below his chin and wiped his forehead. Lyla did not miss a beat. She ran to him as fast as she could. The sudden embrace surprised him.

"Lyla!" The doctor fell to his knees and cried out as he held his daughter close.

Lyla let him squeeze her, "Where's Mom?" The words hardly squeaked out.

The doctor squeezed his daughter harder, and she could feel him shake the answer into her hair. "I'm so grateful you survived."

"*The Penny Dreadful* saved me," Lyla said.

Deep beneath the waves, something old began to stir, its slumber disturbed by chaos upon the ocean's surface. It woke up hungry.

CHECK OUT OTHER GREAT
DEEP SEA THRILLERS

THE BREACH
by Edward J. McFadden III

A Category 4 hurricane punched a quarter mile hole in Fire Island, exposing the Great South Bay to the ferocity of the Atlantic Ocean, and the current pulled something terrible through the new breach. A monstrosity of the past mixed with the present has been disturbed and it's found its way into the sheltered waters of Long Island's southern sea.

Nate Tanner lives in Stones Throw, Long Island. A disgraced SCPD detective lieutenant put out to pasture in the marine division because of his Navy background and experience with aquatic crime scenes, Tanner is assigned to hunt the creeper in the bay. But he and his team soon discover they're the ones being hunted.

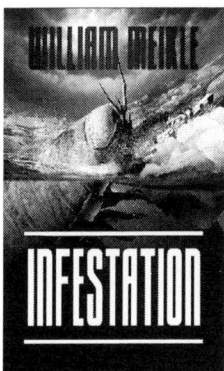

INFESTATION
by William Meikle

It was supposed to be a simple mission. A suspected Russian spy boat is in trouble in Canadian waters. Investigate and report are the orders.

But when Captain John Banks and his squad arrive, it is to find an empty vessel, and a scene of bloody mayhem.

Soon they are in a fight for their lives, for there are things in the icy seas off Baffin Island, scuttling, hungry things with a taste for human flesh.

They are swarming. And they are growing.

"Scotland's best Horror writer" Ginger Nuts of Horror

"The premier storyteller of our time." - Famous Monsters of Filmland

CHECK OUT OTHER GREAT DEEP SEA THRILLERS

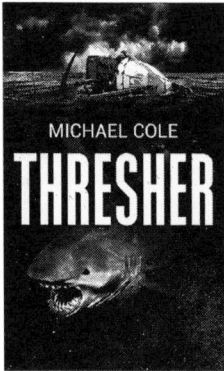

THRESHER
by Michael Cole

In the aftermath of a hurricane, a series of strange events plague the coastal waters off Florida. People go into the water and never return. Corpses of killer whales drift ashore, ravaged from enormous bite marks. A fishing trawler is found adrift, with a mysterious gash in its hull.

Transferred to the coastal town of Merit, police officer Leonard Riker uncovers the horrible reality of an enormous Thresher shark lurking off the coast. Forty feet in length, it has taken a territorial claim to the waters near the town harbor. Armed with three-inch teeth, a scythe-like caudal fin, and unmatched aggression, the beast seeks to kill anything sharing the waters.

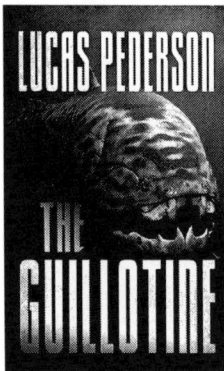

THE GUILLOTINE
by Lucas Pederson

1,000 feet under the surface, Prehistoric Anthropologist, Ash Barrington, and his team are in the midst of a great archeological dig at the bottom of Lake Superior where they find a treasure trove of bones. Bones of dinosaurs that aren't supposed to be in this particular region. In their underwater facility, Infinity Moon, Ash and his team soon discover a series of underground tunnels. Upon exploring, they accidentally open an ice pocket, thawing the prehistoric creature trapped inside. Soon they are being attacked, the facility falling apart around them, by what Ash knows is a dunkleosteus and all those bones were from its prey. Now...Ash and his team are the prey and the creature will stop at nothing to get to them.

CHECK OUT OTHER GREAT DEEP SEA THRILLERS

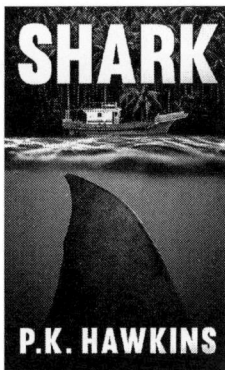

SHARK: INFESTED WATERS
by P.K. Hawkins

For Simon, the trip was supposed to be a once in a lifetime gift: a journey to the Amazon River Basin, the land that he had dreamed about visiting since he was a child. His enthusiasm for the trip may be tempered by the poor conditions of the boat and their captain leading the tour, but most of the tourists think they can look the other way on it. Except things go wrong quickly. After a horrific accident, Simon and the other tourists find themselves trapped on a tiny island in the middle of the river. It's the rainy season, and the river is rising. The island is surrounded by hungry bull sharks that won't let them swim away. And worst of all, the sharks might not be the only blood-thirsty killers among them. It was supposed to be the trip of a lifetime. Instead, they'll be lucky if they make it out with their lives at all.

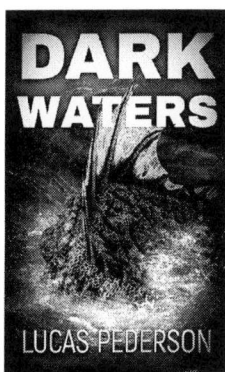

DARK WATERS
by Lucas Pederson

Jörmungandr is an ancient Norse sea monster. Thought to be purely a myth until a battleship is torn a part by one.

With his brother on that ship, former Navy Seal and deep-sea diver, Miles Raine, sets out on a personal vendetta against the creature and hopefully save his brother. Bringing with him his old Seal team, the Dagger Points, they embark on a mission that might very well be their last.

But what happens when the hunters become the hunted and the dark waters reveal more than a monster?

Made in the USA
Middletown, DE
20 November 2018